THREE SURVIVED

BY ROBERT SILVERBERG

Nonfiction

Science Fiction

THREE SURVIVED

by Robert Silverberg

HOLT, RINEHART AND WINSTON

New York   Chicago   San Francisco

THREE SURVIVED

1

TOM RAND was in his cabin when the spaceship blew its overdrive. One moment he was standing next to his bunk, looking over some work he was doing. The next moment he was flat on his face, wondering what was going on.

He shook the grogginess out of his skull and sat up. He heard alarm sirens wailing. Signal lights flashed on the cabin wall. DANGER! DANGER!

The other lights in the cabin faded. Then they came on again, much brighter than before. And faded. And got bright again. And faded once more.

The ship's gravity went cockeyed next. Everything that wasn't nailed down started to fly around. That included the passengers. Tom Rand felt himself rushing toward the ceiling. He reached up and let his arms take the shock of the collision.

Then the emergency gravity took control. Rand fell back to the floor. The lights stopped flickering.

But he knew that the ship's troubles weren't over. Its troubles were just beginning, and the big question was how bad the troubles were.

And the answer was, very bad.

A low humming sound came throbbing through the cabin wall. It grew higher and higher in pitch until it became a thin, sharp scream. Just when the sound was unbearable, it stopped. And the starship *Clyde F. Bohmer* came snapping out of special space with a jolt that made Tom Rand's eyeballs jiggle.

We've had it, Rand thought.

We aren't going to get home on *this* ship.

Things grew quiet for a moment. Rand picked himself off the floor and grabbed for his cabin phone. With shaky fingers he punched the INFO button.

"What happened?" he asked.

"We have suffered a failure in the main overdrive generator," said the master computer's calm voice. "The result has been total destruction of the front section from Compartments 10 through 14."

"Are you saying that half the ship has blown up?"

"Not exactly half," the computer replied. "In terms of the actual percentage of destruction, about 38 per cent of—"

"Never mind," said Rand. "What shape is the overdrive unit in?"

"The overdrive unit is a complete loss. The voyage has been interrupted."

"Interrupted? You bet!" Rand couldn't bring himself to laugh at the computer's choice of words.

If the overdrive was gone, the computer—the ship's brain—would be the one to know. And if the overdrive was gone, there was no way they could reach Earth. They'd starve to death first.

Overdrive is what gets you from star to star without having to spend your whole life making the trip. A spaceship blasts off from a planet using ordinary rocket drive, but after a couple of days it switches to overdrive. The overdrive pushes the ship out of the regular universe and into special space.

You travel fast in special space. Instead of taking ten or twenty years to go from one star to another, you do it in two or three months. The universe is a big place, and overdrive is the only way to get around it in a hurry.

But a spaceship's overdrive is a complicated gadget. Sometimes it decides to blow up, nobody knows why.

And when it does—

It had happened aboard the *Clyde F. Bohmer,* which was making a hop back to Earth from the distant planet Rigel IV. It had happened without warning, and it had happened fast. Now the ship had been knocked out of special space and crippled.

"What about casualties?" Rand asked.

The computer hummed for an instant. Usually it gave answers without a pause, but right now it had plenty of work to do in all parts of the ship. Rand, who was a space engineer by trade, couldn't blame it if its timing was a little slow right now.

It said, "The air loss was serious in Compartments 8 and 9. Emergency walls are in place and new air supplies have been pumped in. Eight men are injured or dead there. The officers' bridge was destroyed: no survivors known. Engine room destroyed: several survivors, condition serious. Some passengers unharmed although deaths have been observed. Radon clouds are causing dangers in lower levels of the ship. Lifeships 3, 7, 8 are ready for use. Some of the remaining lifeships are damaged and not in working order. Computer section functioning and—"

Rand put the phone down. He had heard what he needed to know.

Now he had to get into action.

The ship was a wreck. And of the 38 men who had been on board when they set out from Rigel IV, possibly 10 were still alive. And most of those weren't in very good shape. Rand counted up the death roll:

Six officers, all of them dead.

Twelve passengers, "some unharmed," according to the computer's first report from the scanning pickups, but "deaths have been observed."

There had been twenty crewmen. A dozen of them had been up front in the engine room. Most of them had probably been killed in the moment of the blowup. Probably all. The computer had said, "Several survivors, condition serious," but maybe the computer was confused. Even computers could get confused when something as bad as this hit a ship. Those men had to be dead up there.

Eight other crewmen had been in Compartments 8 and 9. They hadn't felt the full fury of the explosion. But those eight men had had a heavy dose of exposure to space before the emergency walls moved into position. They were as good as dead, Rand figured. Some of them might still be living, but not for long.

He decided that he was lucky to be alive.

Now what, though?

The only thing that made sense to do was to abandon ship. Get off it in a hurry, Rand thought, before something else blows up. Get off and head for the nearest planet where there might be a rescue signal beacon.

It was a waste of time even to think about making repairs. The ruined ship didn't stand a comet's chance of getting to Earth or anywhere else. With the overdrive gone, the *Clyde F. Bohmer* could only drift helplessly in space.

Rand knew where the lifeships were located. He was the kind of practical man who always checked out things like that when he boarded a spaceship.

There was a lifeship just up the passageway from his cabin.

First, though, he had to see what he could do for the other survivors. If there were any survivors.

He pushed open his cabin door and headed out into the passageway to have a look around.

2

A HOT CLOUD of oily gray smoke hit him in the face the moment he stepped out of his cabin. It stung his nostrils and made his eyes start to weep.

Radon, Rand thought in sudden fear.

He remembered that the computer had told him, "Radon clouds are causing dangers in lower levels of the ship." Radon, a radioactive gas, set free somehow by the explosion in the overdrive generator—deadly poison in the passageways!

He flung his arm across his face and ducked back inside his cabin. Then his moment of panic passed. He was still alive; that meant he couldn't have stepped into a radon cloud. If the smoke out there had been radon, he would be dead now. It was that simple.

Probably the radioactive gas was a danger only on the lower levels. That was what the computer had said. Rand realized that the computer would have taken steps to keep the radon from spreading up here to his part of the ship. Every level must be sealed now.

The smoky cloud in the passageway, then, was

most likely plain old smoke, of the kind that the human race had known for a million years. That was better than having radon out there. But it still wasn't good news. It told him that the ship was now on fire, along with all its other troubles.

He had to go out there, though. He opened his door a second time and forced himself into the dense wall of thick smoke.

Rand knew what his first two stops would have to be. First, Professor Loder's cabin. Then, Number Six Hold, where the cargo of anti-virus drugs was stored. Professor Loder and those drugs were the only two really important things aboard this ship. They had to be rescued, if anything at all got rescued.

Rand didn't have any fancy ideas about his own importance. He was important mainly to himself. He was just a skilled space engineer who had been working for a while in a lab on Rigel IV, and who now was on his way home to Earth.

He wanted very much to get out of this mess alive. But he knew that it wouldn't be any great loss to anyone else if he didn't.

Professor David Loder, though, was the great man of anti-virus research. He had spent the last five years on Rigel IV, trying to develop a drug to deal with a deadly virus disease. The disease was plaguing Earth's colonists on a dozen different planets.

Now Dr. Loder was going home to Earth to test his drug. Once the drug won approval on Earth, it could be shipped to the planets where the virus epidemics were raging.

No other man could have produced that cargo of drugs. Professor Loder and his work spelled the difference between life and death for whole planets. Tom Rand meant to see to it that those years of work hadn't been wasted.

Choking and gasping, he made his way through the smoke-filled passageway, trying not to breathe very often or very deeply. He could hardly see a thing. Tears were streaming down his cheeks as the smoke went to work on his eyes.

Professor Loder was in Cabin Fifteen. Rand found the right door and banged on it with his fists.

No answer came.

He banged again, harder. Still no sound from the other side. After a moment he tried the door. It wasn't locked. He shoved it open and went in.

"Professor Loder!" he called.

The professor was there, all right. Rand saw the small, white-haired man huddled at his desk. His head was slumped forward. A pencil was tightly clutched in his fingers. He wasn't moving.

Rand crossed the cabin in three quick steps. "Professor?" he said hopefully. "Professor Loder?"

He shook the little man's bony arm. Loder's head wobbled, but he didn't wake up.

"Professor Loder!" Rand shouted, as though he could call the great scientist back from the dead by yelling at him. "Snap out of it, professor!"

Loder must have been at work when the sudden shift out of special space had come. The jarring shock had been too much for the frail old man.

Rand went through the routine of checking the professor's pulse, of trying to find some spark of life somewhere. It was useless.

"Is he dead?" a quiet voice asked.

Rand looked around and scowled in disgust. Anthony Leswick stood by the door.

"Yes, he's dead," Rand snapped. He felt like adding, "And *you're* still alive. There isn't any justice in the universe, is there?" But he didn't say it.

Of all the people Rand didn't feel like meeting right this minute, Leswick led the list. Rand had been bugged by Leswick since the beginning of the voyage. He didn't like the first thing about the man. He couldn't stand Leswick's pale, skinny face or his little shiny eyes or his high-pitched voice. And he really despised the so-called "science" that Leswick claimed to be an expert in. *Metaphysical Synthesis.* What kind of science was that?

No kind of science at all, Rand thought. Just some big-sounding words, adding up to absolutely nothing. *Metaphysical Synthesis!* An empty science, a zero science. A phony science.

"Most of the others are dead too," the thin man

10

in the doorway said. "I've been checking all the cabins. It's a great tragedy, isn't it? Luckily, when the explosion came I was—"

"Yes," Rand said tightly. "Suppose you get yourself out of my way now. I want to check on the drug cargo."

He shouldered past Leswick and out into the passageway, feeling hollow and angry inside. It wasn't right, he told himself. For a genius like David Loder to be killed, and somebody like Anthony Leswick to survive—

All during the trip Leswick had been talking up Metaphysical Synthesis. He even gave a lecture on it one night. He had a whole string of degrees from colleges and universities on Earth, but Rand wasn't impressed by that. What counted was what Leswick said, not what degrees he could flash around. And what he said struck Rand as a load of nonsense.

Metaphysical Synthesis, as far as Rand could figure it out, was a mixture of a lot of things. It was a study that tried to tie together history, anthropology, psychology, sociology, and half a dozen other ologies. Everything that went into Metaphysical Synthesis was pretty fuzzy, and what came out was even fuzzier. As an engineer, Rand liked things to have exact rules.

The speed of light was an exact thing. The pull of gravity was an exact thing. The power of a spaceship's drive unit was an exact thing. You could measure and calculate all those things and know where you were and where you were heading.

But to patch together a bunch of foggy and confused subjects that had no exact rules at all, and claim that you'd found the secrets of the universe —no. Rand couldn't buy one bit of that. What bugged him most of all was how smug and cocky Leswick was about his so-called "science." He acted as if he knew it all.

And Leswick was still alive, though David Loder was dead. It wasn't fair! It wasn't fair!

Swallowing his anger, Rand stumbled through the smoke to the end of the passageway. In a few moments he came to the hatch that led to the ship's inner service shaft. His only way of getting to the storage hold and the drugs was down that shaft. Even with Loder dead, the drugs still might save millions of lives.

But the hatch was closed. And it wouldn't open.

Frowning, Rand tugged on the handle. When that failed to do anything, he pressed the emergency release knob. The hatch still didn't open.

Instead, a red light went on over it, and the voice of the ship's computer came from a loudspeaker:

"This hatch is closed for reasons of safety."

"I know," said Rand. "But I've got to get down there to save those drugs!"

"Dangerous radioactive gases have been released

in the lower levels. All connecting hatches have been sealed. This prevents spread of the gases to the upper levels."

"That makes sense," Rand told the computer. "But there's important cargo down there. There may even be some live human beings. Can you tell me if the radon has reached the storage hold?"

"The storage hold is not yet affected by the spread of radon."

"Okay, then. This shaft will take me straight there, won't it? If there's no radon here, and none there, then it won't do any harm to open the hatch. Right?"

"All connecting hatches must remain sealed."

Arguing like this with the computer made him angry. "Listen, you dumb machine. I just explained to you why it's safe to open this hatch! Open it up!"

"Is that a direct order?"

"It sure is," Rand yelled.

"Direct orders can be accepted only from officers of the ship."

"All the officers are dead. You told me so yourself." Rand pounded his fists on the hatch in fury. Then an idea struck him. "Since the officers are dead, command of the ship goes to the civilian who knows most about running a spaceship. That's me. I'm your new captain. I order you to open this hatch. If you say no once more, it'll be mutiny!"

The computer's highly logical mind thought that over for a moment. Then it said, "The order is accepted."

"Thank you," Rand said sarcastically, as the hatch swung open.

3

THERE WAS less smoke in the service shaft than there was in the hall. Rand was glad to breathe some more-or-less fresh air again. He climbed into the shaft and the hatch closed behind him.

Metal rungs lined the wall of the shaft. Rand scrambled down rung by rung to the level where the storage holds were located. The hatch here was sealed too, of course.

One of the computer's scanning pickups was mounted over the hatch. "This is Captain Rand," he said to it. "Open up, fast!"

The hatch opened. Rand jumped through, into the passageway.

There was plenty of smoke here, too. He looked around, trying to find the storage hold. He had never been down in the storage level before, and he didn't know his way around. But the doors here were numbered in the high thirties. The storage hold must be far down the passage, near the damaged end of the ship.

It was hard to see with all the smoke in the air.

He knew he didn't have much time. He started to trot.

A huge figure appeared suddenly out of the dimness ahead and blocked Rand's way. The big man put up one gigantic arm like a traffic cop telling a motorist to halt.

"Where you think you going, fella?"

"Get out of my way, will you?" Rand said impatiently. "I'm in a hurry."

"Well, slow down. There ain't nothing down there you need to see," the big man rumbled.

He looked more like a gorilla than a man. He was at least half a foot taller than Rand, and Rand wasn't small. His clothes were torn and stained with grease. His face and his thick red hair were blackened by smoke. He didn't seem to have shaved in a month. Beads of sweat ran down into his bright blue eyes.

The big man was a deckhand, one of the crewmen who did the dirty jobs in the engine room. Jetmonkeys, they were called. You didn't need much brain to be a jetmonkey, only lots of muscle. But this one was no monkey. He was more like an ape.

It figures, Rand thought, that this rockhead would be the only survivor of the engine crew. Just a big hunk of walking meat that hardly rates as a human being.

The man kept his hand pressed casually against Rand's chest, holding him back.

"I told you I'm in a hurry," Rand said again. He grabbed the other man's thick wrist with both his hands and tried to wrench it away. But the jet-monkey's arm didn't budge.

"You ain't in any hurry, mac, really, you ain't," the jetmonkey said. "You can't go but twenty feet more thisaway. Look, I just come from there myself."

"What do you mean, twenty feet?"

The jetmonkey shrugged. "The red wall's down, thisaway. You can't get past that nohow. So why knock yourself out trying?"

The red wall?

That topped it, Rand thought. That was the chocolate frosting on the cake.

The red wall was ship slang for the radiation shields that were hidden every fifty feet or so in all the passageways. In case hard radiation was spreading through some part of the ship, the red wall would come down to protect the other part.

The computer must have lowered the red wall here a couple of minutes ago, while Rand was scrambling down the shaft. It meant that the deadly radon had reached the storage hold. Anything on the far side of that wall—including of course the drug cargo—was hopelessly hot from a bath of hard radiation.

Rand knew that he could probably make the computer lift the red wall, just as he had made the computer open the hatches. But what for? He'd never come out of the hold alive.

Shoulders slumping in defeat, he turned away. His rescue mission was a total failure. He hadn't been able to save Professor Loder, and he hadn't succeeded in getting the drugs. The overdrive blowup had destroyed everything of value, then.

The jetmonkey looked cheerful, though. He grinned and said, "Hey, smile, mac! You look all used up!"

"I *feel* all used up."

"Why you so gloomy? You ain't dead, are you?"

Rand shook his head angrily. "I might as well be," he said in a low voice. "Might as well."

"Hey! What kinda dumb talk is that?" The big man punched Rand cheerfully. "Come on, mac—let's you and me go find a lifeship and clear outa here. I got a feeling the whole place is goin' to blow."

Rand nodded wearily. "All right, let's go find a lifeship. But first we've got to hunt for survivors." He pointed down the smoke-filled corridor. "Anybody else alive down there?"

"That's pretty funny," the jetmonkey said. "Tell me another joke, now."

"The whole crew's dead, then?"

"All but me, looks like. I always knew I was a lucky one. When the drive blew, I was down back getting some new fuel rods. I heard a big bang and came out for a look. Boom! No engine room! The whole thing gone! Boom!"

"Killed everyone at once?"

"Don't know about killed, but they sure weren't there no more! Except a few, anyway. And they weren't looking so good. I woulda brought them out, but there wasn't no sense in it. Not much left of them, you know?"

They reached the hatch of the service shaft. The jetmonkey tried to pull it open, but it stayed shut.

Rand looked up at the computer's scanner pickup and said, "This is Captain Rand. Open up!"

The hatch opened. The jetmonkey looked at Rand in amazement.

"*Captain* Rand?" he said. "You ain't really the captain, are you?"

Rand managed to smile. "Does this look like a uniform I'm wearing? The captain's dead. So are all the other officers. I got the computer to believe I was the new captain, so it would obey my orders."

"Hey, pretty nice going! You got to be smart to think faster than them brains! Glad to know you, Captain Rand!"

"Rand's enough. What's your name?"

"Dombey," the jetmonkey said. "Bill Dombey."

"Okay, Dombey, let's go find survivors." Rand made a gloomy face. "I know of at least one. A character named Leswick. He's no bargain, but I guess we ought to rescue him."

19

Rand led the way up the hatch and back to the cabin level. The smoke was thicker than ever up there, now.

"Leswick!" he yelled. "Where are you, Leswick?"

"Near Cabin Five," came the faint voice of the Metaphysical Synthesist. "Someone's alive down here!"

"We're coming," Rand called.

He and Dombey stumbled through the smoke. Soon the figure of Leswick could dimly be seen. The philosopher was standing over someone who was covered with blood.

Leswick glanced up. "It's that businessman from the Mars Colony. He's badly hurt, but maybe he'll pull through. We can carry him to the lifeship—"

"Wait," Rand said.

He knelt beside the fallen man and examined him. It was a messy sight. The businessman must have been thrown against the side of the cabin by the shock of the blowup. His head was twisted in a funny way and there was a deep cut behind one ear. Blood was trickling from his lips.

Rand said, "We'll have to leave him behind."

"We can't do that!" Leswick gasped. "That would be murder!"

"Look," Rand said, "this fellow's got a broken neck and maybe a fractured skull too. And we aren't doctors. By the time we could carry him to the life-ship he'd be dead."

"But to abandon him in cold blood—" Leswick protested.

"Do you think he could survive a voyage in a lifeship?" Rand asked. "Forget about him. There's no way we can help him, Leswick. Absolutely no way."

Dombey chimed in, "Yeah. This guy, he's mostly dead right now. We better save room in the life-ship for somebody in better shape."

"And we'd better get going fast," Rand said.

He turned and headed back down the passage-way. Dombey followed him. After a moment, so did Leswick, leaving the dying man where he lay.

Rand looked into another cabin and saw another passenger who was still alive. But he was even more seriously injured than the first one. His eyes were closed and he was making soft groaning sounds. Rand shook his head sadly.

"We'll have to leave him too," he said.

He went to the cabin phone and punched for INFO. "Give me a complete rundown on passen-gers and crew," he ordered. "I want to know how many are still alive, how many dead, how many missing. Check every scanner."

The computer had scanning eyes all over the ship. It constantly drew information from all of them. In a fraction of a second it added up the totals.

"Five men are known to be alive," it reported. "Eighteen men are known to be dead. The remaining fifteen men are missing and believed to be dead."

Rand nodded. "Okay, that settles it. Five men alive—that's the three of us, plus the two injured passengers we just found. There's no sense wasting time looking for anybody else. Leswick, Dombey—let's clear out!"

He rushed down the passageway toward the nearest lifeship.

4

THE LIFESHIP wasn't very much more than a bubble of metal and plastic with a spacedrive attached. It could hold three men comfortably, or four men uncomfortably, and that was all.

Rand made sure the lifeship was in working order by asking the computer to run a quick checkout.

"All systems go," the computer replied.

"Right." Rand pointed a finger at Leswick. "Get inside and strap yourself in."

Leswick started to enter. Suddenly Rand noticed that the little philosopher was carrying a huge book. He must have picked it up from his cabin on the way to the lifeship.

"Hold it, Leswick. What's that book?"

"Something to pass the time while I'm waiting to be rescued," he said. "Why? What's wrong?"

Rand took the book from him and looked it over. His mouth turned down in scorn. The title was, *An Application of Matrix Field Theory to the Cultural Units of Eastern New Guinea*. That didn't tell him a whole lot. He flipped through it and saw that it was the usual Metaphysical Synthesist sort of stuff. A batch of fancy mathematics and long words, adding up to nothing that anybody in his right mind could find useful.

"We'll leave the book behind," Rand said.

"No!" Leswick protested. "What right have you—"

"The lifeship's small and crowded. This book is heavy. It's just dead weight. We can't afford to drag it along."

Leswick grabbed at it. "You can't just toss it away like that! I need that book! It's important to my work!"

"Aw, let him have it, boss," Dombey boomed. "It don't take up *that* much space."

Rand realized that he was being too hard on Leswick. Maybe the book was silly nonsense. Maybe Metaphysical Synthesis itself was silly nonsense. But this was no time to set himself up as the judge of that. He was letting his prejudices get a little too much control over him.

"Okay," Rand said. "Here."

He flipped the book back to Leswick, who caught it clumsily in the pit of his stomach. Leswick tucked the big book under his arm. He swung open the airlock hatch and stepped into the lifeship.

From somewhere deep in the mother ship came the rumblings of a far-off explosion. The computer's voice said, "The fire has reached the fuel storage chambers. Best procedure for survivors is to abandon ship at once."

"You bet," Rand said. "We don't need a computer to help us figure that one out!"

Dombey climbed in after Leswick, and Rand followed him. He yanked down the handle that sealed the lifeship's airlock. Then Rand strapped himself down on the chair in front of the control panel. The other two men climbed into acceleration couches just behind him.

The voice of the computer said, "To achieve exit from the mother ship, press the red knob on the keyboard before you."

Rand looked at the knob. He didn't need the computer's help for that one, either. The knob was plainly marked as the blastoff control. The hard part of the job would come later—when they were on their own, traveling through space.

He wouldn't have any computer to give him advice then. The computer would still be aboard the *Clyde F. Bohmer*. Maybe it could direct him by radio for a little while, but not for long. The *Clyde F. Bohmer* was going to blow up any minute.

Rand suddenly began to sweat. Fear sent cold trickles of perspiration down his sides. Sweat pasted his close-cut hair together into little spikes. For the first time since the trouble began, he was really worried.

Three lives—including his own—lay in his hands.

And he had never piloted any sort of spaceship before.

"We'd better take off, shouldn't we?" Leswick said nervously. "I mean, the ship is in danger of exploding. Why are we staying here? Is there any problem?"

"Yeah, boss, you having trouble?" Dombey asked.

"None at all," Rand forced himself to say. "Everything's okay. I've got matters well under control."

And to his surprise he realized he was speaking the truth. Channels of his mind that he had thought were long closed by rust suddenly opened brightly.

He had never piloted a spaceship, that was true enough. But he had basic knowledge, a grasp of theory. He knew how a spaceship worked, and why. And he knew more than enough math to compute a sort of orbit to the nearest planet.

Maybe it wouldn't be the kind of slick job a real space pilot would do. But the orbit he worked out would get them where they wanted to go. So things *were* well under control. . . .

He hoped.

With fingers that were calm and steady, Rand reached up and pressed the knob that would shoot the lifeship out of the dying *Clyde F. Bohmer*.

The knob passed a signal along to the catapults mounted in the walls around the lifeship. The catapults pushed the lifeship forward. At the same time a big hatch slid open in the outer skin of the mother ship.

The lifeship shot forth into space.

Automatically the computer turned the lifeship's engines on. A surge of power sent the little vessel streaking out into the darkness of space.

"We're on our way," Rand said.

He didn't feel much of a thrill. He had hoped to be piloting Professor David Loder to safety, along with the cargo of precious drugs. But Loder was dead and the drugs were ruined. Out of all that had been aboard the spaceship, he was saving only himself and two others. None of us really matters at all, Rand thought. I'm just an engineer—we're a dime a dozen. And Leswick is a worthless little cockeyed philosopher. And Dombey's a moron of a jetmonkey who probably can't even read or write. What a cargo! Just a load of dead weight!

"You know where we're going, huh?" Dombey asked.

"Sure thing," said Rand.

He wiped the sweat from his forehead. It was running down into his eyes and bothering him.

The lifeship was still in radio contact with the mother ship's computer. Rand said, "How many planets are within range of this lifeship?"

The computer answered, "Three. They belong to the solar system of a star numbered GGC 8788845 in the latest catalog. A rescue beacon was constructed on the second planet of the system in the year 2432."

"Fine," said Rand. "I want you to calculate an orbit for me that'll bring this lifeship down right next to the beacon."

The computer was silent. Rand imagined the electronic impulses racing around inside its complicated machinery. Two or three minutes went by.

"How's that orbit coming?" he asked. "It shouldn't have taken you this long."

The computer made no reply.

"Answer me," Rand said. "This is Captain Rand speaking. I'm giving you a direct order: feed me that orbit at once."

Silence.

"Do you hear me?"

More silence.

"I think the big brain's in trouble," Dombey said. "It oughta be talking to you, boss. Why ain't it answering?"

5

RAND DIDN'T say anything. Suddenly he felt the air in the lifeship cabin growing warm. He could hear the air conditioners working hard to keep the temperature down. He began to realize what must have happened.

He switched on the rear viewscreen.

The screen lit up and flickered wavily for a moment. Then the image focused. Against the blackness of space there was a sprinkling of tiny bright stars. And in the foreground blazed a brand new star that wasn't listed in any of the star catalogs.

It wasn't a star. It was what had been the *Clyde F. Bohmer.*

"Take a look at the ship," Rand said. He pointed toward the rear screen.

"Where?" Leswick said. "I don't see any ship."

"It's that bright star right in front. That's what happens when a spaceship's fuel storage chambers explode. There's nothing left of that ship but atoms."

Leswick shuddered. "We got away just in time!"

As they watched, the fiery glow dimmed and

faded. In a minute or two the explosion was over and nothing could be seen. The air in the cabin was cool again.

"The computer is gone too, of course," Rand said. "It can't work out an orbit now. We're completely on our own."

"Can you land the ship yourself?" Leswick asked.

Rand shrugged. "I can try."

Trying to land a ship without a computer's help was a tough assignment. The problem was that both you and the place where you wanted to land were in motion. You had to aim your ship at the place where the planet was going to be when you planned to get there.

It was something like firing a gun at a moving target. It's important to allow for the ground your target will cover before the bullet reaches it.

Of course, it's a much harder trick to aim a spaceship at a planet than to aim a rifle at a rabbit. Even a little lifeship like this one could reach pretty fantastic speeds. Just a tiny error in the calculations, and Rand would fail to connect with the planet. He might miss it and go right on past.

A different kind of error in the calculations and he'd be traveling too fast when landing time came. The lifeship might slam into the planet at high speed and crack up. A ship in space is different from a rifle bullet, that way. It doesn't matter how fast the bullet is going, as long as it gets to the right place at the right time. But a spaceship has to slow its speed down to zero miles per hour when it lands.

Otherwise—look out!

Rand found some chart paper on a shelf in the lifeship. He also found a little pocket computer. It wasn't much more than a sort of adding machine, but he needed all the help he could get.

He grabbed a pencil and started to write down some numbers.

"Hand me that chartbook," Rand said. "Let's see if I can find out anything useful."

The lifeship's chartbook was a bulky volume that gave information about all the planets that human beings had ever explored. Rand hunted for the star numbered GGC 8788845 and found it quickly. There wasn't much information there—but it would have to be enough.

The chartbook said that star GGC 8788845 was about the same size and astronomical type as Earth's own sun. Good. It wouldn't have been pleasant to have to land on a planet of a dwarf star, where the temperature would be close to absolute zero. Or to land on a planet of one of the hot blue-white stars, where they might get fried instantly.

GGC 8788845 had three planets. The middle one was the one that had the rescue beacon. The chartbook said that it was an Earth-type world with an atmosphere that human beings could breathe. That was another headache they would avoid. They

31

wouldn't need to bundle up in spacesuits while they searched for the rescue beacon.

Rand got to work.

It was terribly quiet in the lifeship cabin. The only sound was the scratching of Rand's pencil as it moved rapidly across the chart paper. Leswick and Dombey were silent, but they looked over Rand's shoulders, trying to see what he was doing.

Neither of them had any idea of what was going on, of course. They could never have begun to land the lifeship without him, Rand knew.

The orbit took shape. Rand's instruments told him how far it was from the lifeship's present position to the planet with the rescue beacon. He already knew how fast the lifeship was able to travel. What he needed to figure out was the speed that the planet was going in its own orbit.

Once he knew that, he could work out an orbit for the lifeship that would match the planet's orbit. He would bring the lifeship closer and closer to the planet, until ship and planet were traveling in the same orbit. Then he'd make rendezvous and land—if his luck held out.

The chartbook gave him some figures about the planet's orbit. He was able to calculate the rest. He made plenty of mistakes as he worked. Soon the chart paper was blurred and smeared and messy from all the erasing he was doing.

But Rand's confidence was growing. He felt sure

that the orbit he was working out was a good one, and would get them safely down.

"Okay," Rand said finally, a long while later. The lifeship had been moving in a big circle through space while he was working. Now he checked out his figures one last time. "We can start our landing approach," he announced.

The lifeship's engine controls were like the keyboard of a typewriter. Rand let his fingers rest lightly on the keys while he looked over the instruction panel. At last he felt ready to begin. He started to tap out his orders.

"Hand me that chartbook again," Rand said. "While we're heading for the planet, maybe I can figure out where that rescue beacon is."

The chartbook told him that Earthmen had visited this planet only once—fifty years before. An Exploration Corps team had stopped off there for a quick visit. They had collected information about the three worlds of the star GGC 8788845. They had also taken the time to set up a rescue beacon on one of those worlds.

The Exploration Corps was trying to set up rescue beacons all through the galaxy. That way, space-wrecked travelers anywhere would have a chance of calling for help.

Rand was gambling that the beacon would still be there after fifty years, and that it would still work right. But he didn't really have much choice.

The lifeship wasn't stocked with fuel for a long voyage. The planet ahead was just about the only one it could have reached.

Let's see, now, Rand thought. The beacon is on the big continent north of the equator and—

Leswick said, "Tell me, does this planet have a name?"

"It's called Tuesday," Rand said, and went on making calculations.

"Tuesday? What a strange name!"

"I didn't name it," Rand muttered.

"But why would anyone call a planet *Tuesday?*"

Rand looked up, annoyed. "It's Exploration Corps rules that every planet has to be named by the survey team that visits it. At first they named the planets for famous men or for cities or countries. That's how we got planets named Kennedy and Columbus and New Shanghai."

"Yes, but—"

"Let me finish, as long as you asked. There are billions of stars, and most of those stars have planets in orbit around them. All the famous names were used up long ago. So now we get planets named Fred and Joe and Sam. There's a planet named Death, and one named Hothouse, and one called Lambchop."

"And a planet named Tuesday," Leswick said.

"Sure. Maybe it's the day the planet was discovered. Or the day the explorers left to go home.

Look, it doesn't matter what the planet's called, or why. What matters is making a safe landing."

Dombey said, "Hey, *today's* Tuesday! Maybe that's good luck—landing on Tuesday on Tuesday!"

Rand smiled faintly. He kept on working, and got the lifeship aimed toward the continent where the rescue beacon had been set up. With luck, he thought, we'll land there.

After that, the next problem was finding the beacon once they had landed. The *Clyde F. Bohmer's* computer could have guided the lifeship to a landing in exactly the right spot. Rand, doing the best he could without the computer, knew he'd be doing well to come down within a thousand miles of the beacon.

One headache at a time, though, he told himself.

And the first job was to land the lifeship without getting killed.

6

THEY WERE getting closer and closer to the planet called Tuesday.

The lifeship swung around the planet in an orbit that was almost a circle. Each time around, the ship moved in, getting a little nearer to its goal. Before long it would be close enough to pass through Tuesday's atmosphere. Then Rand would fire the braking jets to slow the ship, and bring it in for a landing.

He was working hard. He couldn't relax for a minute, now. He had to keep checking the orbit, making certain the ship was taking the right path down.

He glanced back at the two men in the acceleration couches. Dombey was completely relaxed. He was grinning, and he was rocking back and forth in rhythm with the pounding of the engines. He looked like he was enjoying himself.

Leswick was more nervous. He was peering at the control board with beady eyes, watching everything Rand was doing.

Rand smiled, but it was a tense smile. The lives

of these two men were in his hands. They could never have piloted this lifeship anywhere. What did they know of orbits and thrust, of jet compensation and mass ratios, and all the rest?

Nothing. Nothing at all.

Their lives depended on Rand's ability to turn book-learning into practical skills. His training in spaceship theory had simply been part of his general education as an engineer. But it was turning out to be awfully important knowledge. Leswick and the big jetmonkey were just dead weight on this trip, Rand thought. Just dead weight.

Leswick said, "How much longer before we reach that planet?"

"Relax," Rand said. "We're on our way."

The planet called Tuesday was rapidly growing in the front viewscreen. Rand felt the ice-cold lump of tension inside him beginning to melt. In its place came a sort of quiet joy, as he realized that his know-how and his logical outlook were going to get them there.

Who said piloting spaceships is tough work, he thought? There's nothing to it! It's a cinch!

Tuesday was close enough now so Rand could see the continent where the rescue beacon was supposed to be. It was a round continent with jagged edges and ocean all around it. A huge river ran on an angle from northwest to southeast. There were some big lakes in the southwest.

The middle of the continent was a deep green color. As though a dense jungle covered everything.

In another few minutes, the lifeship would be landing. Rand couldn't stay at the control panel any longer. He got up and moved across the little cabin toward the empty acceleration couch next to Leswick.

"What's the matter?" Leswick asked.

Rand strapped himself into the acceleration couch. He stretched out on the foamy plastic cushion.

"We're about to land," he said. "I'm letting the automatic pilot bring us down. It may be a bumpy landing, and I want all the padding I can get when we hit."

He hoped all his calculations had been right. There was nothing he could do about it at this point, though, if he'd made a mistake. Right now all they could do was hang on tight and pray.

The lifeship rushed toward the planet.

Tuesday's jungles grew on the viewscreen. The television cameras in the lifeship's nose showed giant trees tightly packed together.

Down—down—

"Here we come!" Rand yelled.

The braking jets were firing now. The lifeship's engines were trying to slow the ship's fall toward the planet. Moment by moment the speed dropped. Down—

Down through the treetops. Rand closed his eyes. He felt the impact as the lifeship smashed through the green roof of the jungle. How fast would they be going when they hit solid ground? *Too* fast, maybe?

The moment of landing arrived.

The lifeship swayed wildly as it sliced into the trees. It bounced from tree to tree, nearly flipped over, and somehow managed to come down right side up.

Hard.

It cracked into the jungle floor and came to rest.

Rand opened his eyes one at a time. He wriggled his shoulders. He lifted his legs. His body seemed to be working right, so he hadn't broken anything. He felt a little shaken up, that was all. For the first time he understood what it might be like to be a scrambled egg.

"Everybody okay back there?" he called. "Dombey? Leswick?"

"That was a bumpy one, boss," Dombey said.

"We made it, didn't we?" Rand unstrapped himself and looked around the cabin. "Hey, Leswick! Leswick?"

The expert on Metaphysical Synthesis looked a little groggy. He seemed a little green in the face, too. Leswick put his hand to his forehead as if trying to wipe away an imaginary spiderweb that covered his eyes. But he said, "I'm still in one piece —I think."

"The ship sure ain't," Dombey said.

Rand nodded. The force of the landing had cracked and dented and split the wall of the lifeship in many places. The lifeship's hatch had popped, and was wide open. Rand swung himself through it and dropped lightly to the ground outside the ship.

The landing had made quite a mess. Out of the ship, and out of the jungle, too.

Huge trees had been snapped off and thrown around like twigs. There was fallen timber everywhere. The braking jets had scorched the ground over a wide area. Tangled vines trailed down from trees that hadn't fallen.

The lifeship had plowed deep into the soft, spongy ground. It had smashed up its landing fins, ruined its jets, and demolished most of its rear assembly. That was one ship that wasn't going anywhere ever again.

But the three passengers had come through the landing in good shape. And that was the important thing, after all.

Dombey came out of the ship after Rand. He took a deep breath. "It smells pretty good," the jet-monkey said. He stood leaning against the ship's battered hull, his legs planted firmly in the turned-up soil, his head thrown back. "Smells just like air —real air. Good place, huh?"

Leswick peered through the open hatch. He said uneasily, "Isn't it dangerous? Should we breathe the air of an unknown world without making some sort of test?"

Rand grinned. "We *are* making a test. We're breathing the air, and it isn't killing us. Risky, but it happens to be the only test we're equipped to make. We're not carrying much in the way of scientific instruments on this ship."

"Well—"

"Anyway," Rand went on, "the ship split open before we had a chance to put spacesuits on. So we were breathing the air right away, and it didn't hurt us. Why make a fuss now?"

"Suppose it does some long-range harm to us?"

"The chartbook says that this planet has air that Earthmen can breathe," Rand replied. "Which means it's mostly nitrogen and oxygen and good things like that, with no poisonous stuff like methane thrown in. And besides that, what metaphysical suggestion would you have for going somewhere else, if the air wasn't good here? The lifeship's wrecked, you know."

Leswick shrugged. "I guess you're right. I don't know."

Rand turned away. He couldn't stand illogical

41

people, and Leswick just didn't like to think logically. Which made Leswick a worse handicap right now than Dombey. Dombey didn't like to think at all—but, unlike Leswick, he was big and strong. No doubt his strength would come in handy while they were searching for the rescue beacon. Rand figured that that was going to be a long, hard search.

He surveyed his team. It wasn't too promising.

Leswick hardly looked like the type who would do well at jungle exploring. He was a small, thin man with graying hair and deep-set, shiny eyes. He looked like the kind who would be hopelessly lost and confused outside a library or classroom.

As for Bill Dombey, Rand had privately started calling him Tarzan—King of the Apes. He was simply a huge good-natured animal. Rand stood a solid five-feet-eleven, but Dombey was more than six inches taller. Despite his size, Dombey managed to move gracefully. His face was broad and open, with thick, honest features.

He looked like a good sort. Just not very bright, that was his only trouble.

Leswick said, "How are we going to find the rescue beacon?"

"It ought to be broadcasting a standard signal modulating a thirty-megacycle carrier," said Rand. "Does that mean anything to you? Well, never mind. What we need to do is rig a detector that will pick up the signal. Then we follow the path the detector points out."

"Do we have such a detector?" Leswick asked.

"I'm going to build one," Rand told him. "I'll use some of the leftover radar parts from the lifeship. We won't be needing the ship any more, so we can rip out whatever will be handy. Once we know where the rescue beacon is, we're going to set out on foot. Got that?"

"And what will we eat?" Leswick asked. "It may take days to reach the beacon! Our food supply—"

Rand said, "It might even take months. We've got some food capsules in the lifeship's survival kit, but they won't last long. After that we start living off the land. We eat whatever we find that looks good to eat."

"But how will we know if it's safe?"

Rand let his breath out in a long angry whoosh. "You're just overflowing with questions today, aren't you, Leswick?"

"I'm sorry. It's just that I like to be careful in everything I do."

"Well, we'll test the food the same way we tested the air—by trying it. If something doesn't make us sick the first time, we'll keep on eating it. Luckily, I know how to build a machine to give us pure water. But we'll have to feel our way with the meat and the vegetables and take our luck."

"If you say so."

"I say so, yes. What else can we do? Anyway," Rand said, "there isn't all that much danger of catching a horrible disease on a strange planet. It turns out that Earthmen get sick only from Earth-type germs. The bugs here will probably have as little interest in us as we would in them."

"Very well," Leswick said.

"There's one more thing we ought to settle now," said Rand. "We're going to find ourselves in situations where somebody's going to have to make decisions for the three of us. And fast. We won't be able to stop to take a vote."

"You're saying we ought to pick a leader, then?"

"You bet. A man to give orders when orders need to be given. And I think I ought to be the man, since I'm the only one here with any technical skills. What do you say?"

"It suits me," said Leswick. "You seem to know what you're doing. I'll take your orders."

Dombey remained silent.

"What about you, Tarzan?" Rand asked.

"What about what?"

"We're choosing a leader for this little expedition."

Dombey shrugged. "Don't matter none to me. But I'm gettin' pretty hungry. We goin' to be doin' much more talkin'?"

7

AN HOUR LATER, Rand crouched over a tangled mass of wires and coils, scratching his head in puzzlement. Leswick stood above him with a mild expression of curiosity on his face. Dombey was munching on a greenish, nearly transparent piece of fruit that he had pulled down from a tree.

Rand was tinkering desperately with the equipment he had taken out of the lifeship. He was trying to turn a radar set into a peak-detector in a hurry, and he was having a hard time.

The factory that had made the lifeship must really be old-fashioned, he thought in annoyance. Instead of using printed circuits and plug-in units for the radar set, the designers of the equipment had used dozens of separate components.

Rand had never seen anything like that before, except in science museums. It was practically prehistoric, as electronics gear went. It made his job ten times as hard as it should have been.

But rules were rules. He knew he could come up with the device he needed, sooner or later. He just had to be patient and go one step at a time.

"What seems to be the trouble?" Leswick asked.

"You won't understand if I tell you," Rand snapped.

He felt tense and uncomfortable. The sun was fiercely hot. And there was no shade around the lifeship, because so many trees had been knocked down. He was getting sunburned fast. But he stuck to his work.

He added an extra capacitor. "That might do it," he said, and stood back.

Mystified, Leswick peered at the confusing and confused-looking network of resistors, condensers, and crystal diodes. "How can you tell one thing from another?" he asked. "How do you know what you're doing in there?"

"It's something you learn through sweat and toil, friend. Sweat and toil. Two words you probably haven't synthesized into your philosophy yet." Rand slid the copper-shielded case closed with a twitch of his pliers. He picked up the instrument carefully and carried it back inside the ship. Carefully he wired it to the power source and turned it on. It began to hum gently.

So far so good, he thought. We'll use our wits and we'll make out okay. Just call me—Robinson Caruso, was that his name? The fellow that lived on the island.

He began to tune the detector.

Fifteen minutes later he stepped out of the ship.

He was dripping wet with perspiration and he carried a scribbled-on sheet of paper. He had to look around for a moment before he found the other two.

Dombey had collected an enormous heap of the pale green fruits. He was squatting over them and eating them in big mouthfuls. He appeared to be enjoying them.

Leswick, meanwhile, was on the far side of the ship, leaning against the scaly gray side of an uprooted tree. The Metaphysical Synthesist seemed deep in thought. He looked at least ten million miles away.

"I've found the beacon," Rand announced loudly. "The detector picked up its signal!"

Leswick snapped out of his dreamy trance. "Is it far from here?"

Rand held up the crude map that he had drawn. "It's about four hundred miles due east. Unless I made a mistake in figuring and it's even farther. We'll keep checking the reading as we travel. The detector will work off a battery."

"Four hundred miles! But that's—"

"I know, professor. We aren't going to get there in one afternoon. And so far as I know it's all jungle between here and there. Hot, sticky jungle, full of strange beasts and other nuisances." Rand yawned and wiped away some sweat. "Hey, Tarzan, throw me one of those fruits, will you?"

"Here, boss." Dombey scooped up one of the fruits in his gigantic hand and tossed it to Rand.

He caught it and looked it over. It was pointed at both ends and plump in the middle. Its skin was thin and such a pale green that he could see right through it to the core. Rand shrugged and took a bite.

The fruit was watery and didn't have much taste. Eating it was a little like biting into an unripe tomato. But at least it was cool and wet, and Rand had the feeling that it might be healthy to eat. He finished it in four more bites and spat out the core, a small hard red seed.

"Not bad," he commented. "Nothing great, but I think it'll be useful. Professor, suppose you stop daydreaming and start gathering as many of these as you can reach. They may not grow along our route, and we're going to need every safe kind of food we can find."

Leswick nodded and walked over to one of the trees that grew the pale green fruits. He started to pick them. Good, Rand thought. If the philosopher would do his share of the work, they'd stand a much better chance of making it safely through the jungle to the beacon.

"Tarzan, you come here with me," Rand said. "I want to unload the ship before nightfall. We'll drag out of it everything we can possibly use."

He and Dombey went into the ship.

Rand wondered if Dombey and Leswick would ever realize how lucky they were that he was a trained engineer. They couldn't possibly have survived this long without him.

Dombey, of course, wouldn't stop to think about that. The poor dope was happy to be alive, but he didn't spend much time thinking about such things. Or anything.

Leswick, though, ought to recognize his good luck. He'd be a dead man without me by now, Rand thought. What good was a professor of Metaphysical Synthesis on a jungle planet?

Leswick had said that his special field of study was savage tribes. Well, there might be savage tribes here. But how would he deal with them? He seemed able only to deal with situations in books.

Rand had looked into the book Leswick had brought along. It was full of chapters about cultural arcs and tribal war-patterns and other high-sounding things. There were solid pages of mathematical equations, too. But could Leswick translate any of that into useful knowledge? Rand didn't think so.

Then he shook his head. He told himself that he had no business thinking such things. He had been lucky, too. Lucky that he had been born clever, and not dull-witted like Dombey. Lucky that he had chosen to study engineering, and not something that wouldn't do him any good in a tough situation like this.

But it wasn't right to keep congratulating himself for his own good luck. He told himself to cut it out. If I pat myself on the back much harder, he thought, I'll sprain my shoulder.

"Grab hold of this, Tarzan," he called. "Let's haul it outside."

"Sure, boss, sure." Dombey reached up easily and broke loose a long strip of metal from the cabin wall. That would be useful, Rand knew.

Dombey picked up the heavy piece of metal, grunted, and carried it out of the ship by himself. When he came back in, he grinned, scratched the thick stubble on his cheek, and spat out a mouthful of fruit. He rubbed his stomach happily and belched.

"You know what, boss? Them fruits is pretty good, but I could go for a little beef, now. Something to drink, maybe, too."

"You know what, Tarzan? So could I. But let's finish clearing the ship first."

They worked until it got dark. By then they had ripped out of the ship just about everything that might come in handy in the weeks ahead.

The darkness was spooky and weird. This planet had no moon, and the jungle turned black and frightening after sundown.

Strange noises came out of the distance. Birds made a rasping, harsh chirping sound. Something far away made a loud mooing noise, over and over and over. Another animal made a sound that was midway between the neighing of a horse and the screeching of an owl. It wasn't the kind of sound that made you feel cheerful about spending a night on the planet called Tuesday.

Leswick and Dombey gathered twigs and logs and built a fire near the ship. Meanwhile Rand checked out the survival kit to see how much food and medicine they had. Not much, he discovered.

The fire became a hot, lively blaze. It would help to keep the jungle animals away, Rand figured. Maybe they had never seen fire before. In any case, they wouldn't come close. Especially since the life-ship's rough landing had knocked a big opening in the jungle. The animals wouldn't want to cross that clearing of burned and flattened trees.

"Dinner's ready," Rand called, when the fire was lit.

They squatted by the fire and had a simple meal. Food tablets out of the survival kit, and some of the green fruits Dombey had discovered. Then they went inside the ship to sleep.

This would be the last time they would be sleeping indoors for many weeks. After tonight, they'd be out in the open, sleeping in the jungle.

Rand stretched out on one of the acceleration couches. Dombey, next to him, was already asleep. Leswick was sitting up crosslegged, reading his big book by flashlight. Rand looked sourly at him.

"Why don't you save your eyesight, Leswick? Do your homework some other time!"

"It's an extremely fascinating book," Leswick said. "You ought to read it yourself."

Rand laughed. "Yeah. Maybe I will, some year or other. But not right away."

He closed his eyes. But the light of Leswick's flashlight bothered him. After a few minutes Rand said, "Leswick, do you mind putting out that light? I can't sleep."

"If you'll only let me finish this chapter—"

"The chapter might be a hundred pages long. Put out the light, Leswick."

"But—"

"Put out the light."

Leswick made a clucking sound of annoyance. But he switched the flashlight off.

"Thank you," Rand said.

He wrapped his arms around his head and waited for sleep to take him.

8

SLEEP DIDN'T seem to want him, though. Hours passed, and Rand stayed awake.

Listening.

Thinking.

Worrying.

The jungle sounds echoed through the night. Howls and wails and chirps and screams and roars of fifty different kinds split the air. Booming, bellowing, hissing noises could be heard. It was like trying to sleep in the middle of a zoo.

The animals weren't coming close to the ship. Not yet. The fire kept them at a distance—for now.

But soon the three Earthmen would be far from the ship, sleeping out in the open. How much good would a fire do them then? How long would it be before the jungle beasts got curious?

The jungle beasts weren't Rand's only worry. This planet had intelligent native life. The chartbook said so—but the chartbook didn't go into details. What kind of natives? Cannibals? Headhunters? Or creatures so strange and alien that they couldn't be described?

The lifeship's survival kit included a Thorson thought-converter. That was a device that automatically translated languages into terms that could be understood anywhere. The converter would allow him to speak with Tuesday's natives. But it didn't guarantee that they'd give him a friendly, peaceful reception.

Rand tossed uneasily for hours, wondering how they were going to deal with all the problems ahead. This was going to be a test of their skill, toughness, and energy. He felt that he would have what it took to get through the jungle alive. But how about Dombey? Toughness and energy, yes, but no brains. How about Leswick? No toughness, no energy, and, as far as Rand could see, no skill.

Rand knew that even his own abilities as an engineer could get them only so far and no farther. When a man is facing a deadly jungle beast about to spring, it doesn't matter how good an engineer he is. That man is in trouble. Even cleverness has its limits.

Thoughts like these kept Rand awake almost until morning. At last he slipped into a light doze. Right away, it seemed, the sun came up and woke him.

Blinding rays of sunlight came slanting into the ship, through the broken places in the cabin wall. Rand groaned. He tried to hide from the morning brightness, without any luck.

He sat up, yawned, and rubbed the sleep out of his eyes. He was surprised to find himself alone in the ship. Stumbling to the open hatch, he looked out.

"Good morning," Leswick said. "We've been waiting for you. It's breakfast time."

The smell of roasting meat drifted toward Rand.

Dombey was standing by the fire. He had rigged a spit out of two green forked sticks set upright in the ground, with a third stick laid across them. An animal about the size of a large dog was on the spit, getting cooked. Leswick sat to one side, his big book on his lap.

"How long have you two been up?" Rand asked.

"About an hour," said Leswick. "You looked like you needed the sleep, though."

That's for sure, Rand thought.

He pointed to the animal on the spit. "What's that?"

Leswick said, "It came creeping close to the ship around dawn. Dombey moved fast and caught it with his hands. Then he decided to cook it for breakfast."

Dombey looked up and grinned proudly. "You said you could go for a little beef, boss. Right?"

Rand took a close look at the animal. It was a kind of lizard, he guessed. It had a long scaly tail and six legs with ugly sharp claws.

He wasn't exactly in the habit of eating lizard

steaks for breakfast. But he wasn't exactly in the habit of getting shipwrecked on strange planets, either. And that sizzling meat smelled awfully good.

It tasted awfully good, too. The three men polished the animal off, down to the bones. The flavor was more like chicken than like steak, it turned out. For dessert they had the green fruits.

"Okay," Rand said. "Feast time is over. Now we get down to some work."

It was a busy morning for everybody. Rand put together a water purifier, using equipment he found in the ship. Leswick ripped the covers off the acceleration couches and stapled them along the sides to make sleeping bags. Dombey hammered some strips of metal lining from the cabin wall into crude pots, pans, and dishes.

The sun grew blistering hot in the clearing. The men tried to keep to the shade while they worked, but it wasn't easy. Now and then animals peered at them from the underbrush. They didn't dare to come close, though.

By now the men had taken out of the ship just about anything of any value. Everything was arranged in the clearing. Rand looked their supplies over and said, "We're better off than I thought. We've got plenty of gear. There's only one big thing missing."

"Which is?" Leswick asked.

"Weapons. We're setting out absolutely unarmed

across an unknown jungle planet. That's not so good."

Dombey said, "Well, boss, I got this here knife—"

He showed it. It was a small jackknife that might be all right for skinning animals, but not much else.

Rand shook his head. "We need something a little more powerful at long range. Like a rifle, or maybe a blaster gun. But there's nothing like that in our survival kit, and we can't put a gun together out of what we have. So we'll just have to hope we're lucky about what we run into in the forest."

"We could carve boomerangs," Leswick suggested.

"What's a boomerang?" Rand asked.

"A curved throwing stick, used by hunters of an ancient tribe in Australia, on Earth. There's a discussion about it in my book. A properly aimed boomerang can kill an animal hundreds of yards away. Wait—I'll show you—"

For a moment Rand almost took the notion seriously. He looked at the page Leswick showed him and read what it said about the boomerang. Then he scowled in disgust. This was just the sort of dumb impractical idea you could expect from Leswick. A throwing stick!

"I'm not sure if I understand this," Rand said, "because whoever wrote this book of yours seems to think it's evil to use three short words if ten long ones will do. But it appears to say here that carving boomerangs is an extremely difficult art that takes years of practice. You have to use just the right wood, and cut it at just the right angle. And then you need to spend a couple of years learning to throw the things." He shut the book with a slam and handed it back to Leswick. "I'm afraid we don't have the time. You have any other clever ideas?"

"I was just trying to be helpful," said Leswick.

They would have to get along without weapons, Rand told himself. It didn't matter. Somehow their luck would hold out. They would get to the beacon alive.

Somehow.

Dombey said, "I want to show you something, boss. Found it while you were sleeping."

The big man walked off toward one side of the clearing and into the jungle. Rand followed him. When they had gone about fifty feet Dombey stopped and pointed.

"See that? We got ourselves a road!"

The jetmonkey was right. A path about six feet wide ran through the jungle! Someone—or something—had cut back the shrubbery and hacked away the vines. The path was clearly marked, as if it got pretty heavy traffic. Best of all, it ran due east. Rand had calculated that the rescue beacon lay in that direction.

"Good going," Rand said. "That'll save us a lot

of hard work, if it really keeps running to the east. I wasn't looking forward to chopping a hole in that jungle."

Rand and Dombey returned to the clearing. They were ready to leave, now. Rand looked around. Three or four scrawny bird-like things had already moved into the stripped-down lifeship. They had long purple necks, big bulging eyes, and tails like pieces of striped rope. They strutted around the ship, fluttering their long feathery wings and squawking.

"It's all yours," Rand said to the bird-creatures. Before long, he knew, the jungle would move in and hide the scars of their landing. Vines would wrap themselves around the ship and bury it.

He turned to Dombey and Leswick. "It's getting toward noon. I think we've done all we can here. Let's load up and get ourselves going."

He strapped as much as possible to Dombey's broad back. The jetmonkey didn't complain as Rand loaded the baggage on. Once or twice he grunted.

"That too much for you?" Rand asked.

"I can manage," Dombey said. He took a few staggering steps to prove it.

"Your turn," Rand said to Leswick.

The philosopher didn't object. Rand strapped the bundled-up sleeping bags on his back, and added a load of fruit. Then he hoisted the rest of their gear onto his own back, and Leswick lashed it in place.

Rand was carrying the detector that would lead them to the distant beacon.

"Onward and upward," Rand said. "Let's march!"

9

RAND CHECKED his detector and his compass and set out to the east—toward the rescue beacon. Leswick fell in behind him, and Dombey brought up the rear.

They marched silently for nearly an hour. The path they were following took a twisting route through the jungle, and sometimes it swerved toward the south or north. Once it even seemed to double back on itself and head west. Despite all the curves and turns, though, it still went mainly toward the east. It was a well worn path, lined with stamped-down leaves and twigs.

Rand wondered how long it would be before they met the people who had made the path.

The jungle was tropical, heavy with fog and warm mist. Humming yellow-winged insects circled their heads, and they marched forward through clouds of red gnats. The borders of the path were lined with tall, narrow trees that had scaly bark.

The trees shot up straight for hundreds of feet. They had no branches at all close to the ground. High above the jungle floor they sprouted long branches that bore thick, heavy leaves. Each leaf was the size of a man. The tops of the trees were close together, forming a green canopy.

Every half hour or so there was a light rainfall. But very little of the rain reached the men walking through the jungle. The big leaves of the high canopy caught most of the moisture. Rand could hear the sounds of drizzle pattering against the leaves, even when he felt no raindrops.

Long snaky vines dangled from the high branches. They were like thick ropes, some as thick as a man's arm. Closer to ground level grew shrubs and small trees. The low twisted trees that bore the green fruits seemed to grow all over the jungle.

Leswick was the first to point that out. "I should have known it," he complained. "These fruits are everywhere—and here I am, carrying ten pounds of them on my back!"

"Keep them there," Rand said. "For all we know, this is the last grove of those trees between here and the beacon. We may be sorry later if we throw away the ones you're carrying."

"They grow everywhere," Dombey said suddenly. "He *can* throw 'em away, boss."

Rand chuckled. It wasn't often that Dombey sounded so sure of anything.

"Oh? Have you made a study of the botany here,

Tarzan? Are you *certain* the fruit trees grow all over? How can you know?"

Dombey made an annoyed-sounding grunt. "I just know, is all. Boss, he can throw those things away, honest. He's only gonna get tired from carrying 'em. Believe me, there's plenty more where these came from."

"You hear that, Rand?" Leswick said. "If I don't need to carry them, I don't want to carry them!"

Rand shook his head. "Listen, Leswick, maybe Dombey knows what he's talking about, and maybe not. But until I'm sure that the fruit trees are common all around here, I don't plan to scrap our supply. Ten pounds more or less won't kill you."

"He ain't so strong, boss," Dombey put in. "He don't need to carry them things."

This time Rand got sore. He whirled around and said sharply, "That's enough from you, Dombey! When I need your suggestions I'll come asking for them!"

The big man shrugged and didn't reply. Rand turned front again, and stepped up his pace. Up to now, Dombey hadn't had much to say, and had never put up much of a fuss over anything. Rand couldn't understand why Dombey was being so stubborn over the business of the green fruits.

But Rand didn't like it. If the husky jetmonkey started getting troublesome now—

Rand didn't care for the idea that they were quarreling like this. The way they were going, they'd be at each other's throats in another half an hour. And it was going to take days or weeks or months to reach that beacon.

No one spoke again during the next hour. Rand plodded forward, looking back now and then to make sure the other two were keeping up with him. The path had some rough patches, but it still trended toward the east. He checked the detector near noon. They were heading the right way.

The next bit of trouble came when Rand called a halt for lunch.

"This looks like a good place to take a break," he said. "We'll stop here."

They were in a little natural clearing. A sparkling stream wound down from a low hill not far away. A small tree with fur-covered branches was full of fat round fruits that looked like juicy purple apples. It was a beautiful spot.

But Dombey began to shake his head.

"No, boss," the jetmonkey rumbled. "Don't stop now. Not here."

"Huh? Aren't you hungry?"

"Sure," Dombey said.

"Then why shouldn't we stop now?" Rand demanded, annoyed.

Dombey seemed to search for words. He frowned. His nostrils flickered as he sniffed the air. Then he shook his head again, stubbornly. "Bad to stop here, is all. I don't like it here. I don't know why."

Rand folded his arms and looked around the lovely little clearing. He wondered why Dombey was making all this trouble. He said to Leswick, "Do you want to stop and eat here, professor?"

Leswick nodded. "But if Dombey thinks there's something wrong here, maybe we ought to listen to him."

"Let's go, boss," Dombey said, sounding worried. He walked around nervously in a little circle. "We ought to get out of here. It smells bad."

Rand told himself not to get angry. He forced a grin and said, "All right, Tarzan. We'll humor you. We'll keep hiking until you decide you want to stop. How's that?"

"Just don't like it here," Dombey repeated dimly.

They moved on. After they had gone some thirty feet into the underbrush, Rand turned and looked back into the clearing. A slender, gentle-looking animal had come down into it from the little hill. The creature was something like an antelope, except that antelopes don't usually have six legs. This animal did.

It capered around the clearing for a moment. Then it stretched upward, standing on its hindmost pair of legs, to nibble fruits from the tree with furry branches.

Suddenly Rand gasped.

"Look at that!" he said to Leswick.

An arm was silently slithering out of the inno-cent-looking little stream. The arm was green and narrow and long. It had two sharp claws at one end, like yellow spikes, and some sucker-pads. It stretched like rubber, getting longer and longer and longer as it slid across the ground toward the antelope.

The antelope didn't notice. It was concentrating on knocking a fruit from the lowest branch. The branch was a couple of feet above its head, and it wasn't having much luck.

For a last try, the antelope gathered its six legs together to make a jump at the dangling fruit. And in that moment, the long green arm from the water reached it. The arm wrapped itself tightly around all six of the antelope's hooves. Then it began to pull the antelope toward the stream.

The antelope gave a soft, frightened cry. It was helpless in the green thing's grip.

"Can't we do something?" Leswick asked.

"Not a thing," said Rand unhappily.

They watched as the arm got closer to the stream. With a motion like the cracking of a whip, it roughly yanked the animal along and hoisted it over a big rock at the stream's edge. It pulled the antelope down into the water and out of sight.

The jungle became terribly quiet.

Rand turned away. His lips were dry and his legs felt shaky.

Leswick said hoarsely, "It's a good thing we didn't stop to eat lunch in that clearing."

"Yeah," Rand said. *"Very* lucky."

He could see how it might have been. The three of them sitting under that tree, relaxing, eating. And that awful arm quietly sliding toward them along the ground—

Rand glanced at Dombey. The big man hadn't said anything, not even, "I told you so!" Yet his stubbornness had saved their lives.

How had Dombey known that the clearing was dangerous, Rand wondered. How could he possibly have known?

There was only one answer, Rand decided, as they hiked onward. It was idiot's luck—just a foolish hunch, nothing more. It was only a coincidence that Dombey had felt uneasy in a place of hidden danger. They were lucky they hadn't stopped there, of course. But that didn't mean that Dombey had really known why he was warning them to get away from the place.

It didn't make sense to run this expedition on hunches.

In twenty minutes or so they came to another clearing. "Okay," Rand said. "This isn't as pretty as the other place, but it'll do. We'll eat lunch here."

"Don't want to eat here either," Dombey said. He sounded like a cranky child trying to make trouble for his parents.

"Cut it out," Rand said. "I admit you were right not to want to stop back there. But you can't pull the same stunt everywhere, or we'll never get lunch."

"Sorry, boss. I just don't feel good about staying here."

"Can you tell me why? What's likely to happen?"

"How do I know? I just got this feeling."

"No," Rand said. "That isn't enough. We need a real reason for not stopping, or else we're going to stop. Can you give me a reason—something more solid than just a *feeling?*"

Dombey shook his head.

"Then we eat here," Rand said. He slipped his knapsack off and sat down beside it. Dombey remained standing.

"Do we *have* to eat here, boss?"

"Yes," Rand said. "Even if you don't want to."

Shrugging, Dombey sat down, looking worried and unhappy. They unpacked and got out some food. Rand found that he was a little worried, too. After all, Dombey had seemed to know that the last clearing was dangerous. And here—maybe—

No—it's nonsense, Rand thought.

But he kept glancing off into the jungle to make sure nothing was sneaking up on them. Crackling twigs made him jump. When the wind rustled through the branches, he got up and looked around.

He felt edgy and tense. The picture of that slimy green arm creeping out of the pretty little stream still haunted him.

He didn't see anything in the bushes, though. Except a vine that wound like a snake from bush to bush. Shiny little berries, about the size of grapes, grew on the vine. They were light blue in color and looked juicy and sweet.

Rand picked a few of the berries and said to Dombey, "You don't mind if I try some of these, do you? I have your permission, I hope?"

Dombey said nothing. He just stared.

Rand put one in his mouth. It tasted even better than it looked. "Mmm," he said. "That's good! Sweet as honey! Dombey, you want some?"

"I got the other fruits, boss."

"Suit yourself. Leswick, want to try a few?"

Leswick didn't. Rand ate five or six more. Dombey watched him in an unhappy way, as though the big man thought something might be wrong with the berries. Rand didn't care. He wasn't going to put faith in every one of Dombey's wild hunches.

He had to prove his point about stopping to eat here. He had to operate by logic and common sense, not by hunches and mysterious "feelings." This place was turning out all right, no matter what Dombey said. It would have been a mistake not to

stop here, Rand thought. Even eating the berries—
that would show Dombey this place was okay.

By the time lunch was over, Rand was sure he'd
been right. Nothing unusual had happened to them
in the clearing. They finished eating, packed up, and
went back to the path. Dombey's second hunch
hadn't been as good as his first. Rand was glad about
that.

They started marching again. Not for long,
though.

When they were about half a mile from the place
where they had eaten lunch, Dombey called out,
"Hold it!"

Rand looked back. "What's the matter now?"

"We got to get off the path here," Dombey said.
"Fast!"

10

THIS WAS starting to be a nuisance. Dombey wasn't a silent man any more. Now he seemed to be trying to run the show.

"What did you say?" Rand asked.

Dombey jerked his thumb toward the edge of the jungle. "We gotta get off the path here. Into the woods."

"Are you going to make trouble every step of the way?" Rand asked. "This is the third time in the last two hours that you've stopped us, Dombey. We're never going to get there if—"

"No, boss!" A look of sheer agony passed like a cloud across Dombey's face. He struggled hard to find words and get them out. "Boss, we *gotta* get off the path! Right now!"

"You said that when we stopped for lunch. Both times."

"The first time he was right," Leswick pointed out.

"That was the first time. A lucky hunch, nothing more. But if he's going to get itchy about something mysterious every little while—" Rand said.

It was a matter of principle, he realized. His leadership of the group was at stake. Either he made the decisions, using his intelligence, or Dombey did—using guesswork.

Rand glanced at Leswick to find out where the philosopher stood in the argument. But Leswick's face completely hid his feelings.

"We *aren't* getting off the path," Rand said firmly. "And I'll give the orders in this party, Dombey. Remember that. I'll give the orders."

A new expression entered Dombey's eyes. It was one that Rand had never seen there before. The big man didn't look easy-going and good-natured any more.

"You ain't giving the orders no more," Dombey said in a low growl of a voice. "We get off this path. Right now."

He moved toward Rand. He was as agile as a big cat, in spite of the heavy load of gear strapped to his back.

"Get away, Dombey!" Rand ordered. "Keep back!"

But the huge man kept approaching. His fist was clenched, and he was swinging his arm around to throw a punch. Rand brought an arm up to block the blow. Dombey's punch caught him just below the elbow. Rand's arm went numb.

"Leswick!" Rand yelled. "Pull him back! Get him away from me!"

It was foolish to think that Leswick could be of any use against Dombey, Rand knew. Leswick didn't offer help. He stepped back instead. And Dombey closed in.

A punch slammed into Rand's stomach. He tried to fight back, but it was like fighting off a hurricane. Dombey grazed Rand's jaw with a flat-handed slap that left him spinning dizzily. He followed with a head-rattling swipe to Rand's right shoulder.

He's gone crazy, Rand thought. He's running wild!

But there was a strange look in Dombey's eyes, and it wasn't a look of insanity. In the middle of the struggle, Rand saw that look. It was the look of a man who knew what he was doing.

"Stop it!" Rand cried. "Dombey, cut it out!"

He tried to back away, but Dombey wasn't letting him go anywhere. The jetmonkey grabbed him with one hand. Rand managed to land a weak punch on Dombey's chest, and then Dombey slapped him again, just once, very hard, on his left cheekbone.

Rand's head wobbled and his knees went out from under him.

He started to sag toward the ground. Dombey caught him. Rand felt as if he had begun to fly. Dombey was lifting him, swinging him through the air, dumping him over his broad shoulder.

Then Rand blanked out completely.

He woke up feeling as if a steamroller had hit him. He was lying on a thick carpet of sweet-smelling leaves, under a canopy of branches far overhead. The knapsack he had been carrying was sitting beside him.

Leswick and Dombey stood nearby. Dombey was completely calm, showing no hint of his earlier rage. Leswick looked away guiltily when Rand glared at him.

Slowly, painfully, Rand got to his feet. He was aching in a dozen places. His two companions watched him without saying a word.

"Where are we?" he asked.

Leswick said, "About fifty feet from where you and Dombey had the fight."

"I feel like I've been out cold for days."

"About five minutes, no more," the Metaphysical Synthesist said. "Dombey tried to be careful when he hit you."

"Nice of him," Rand muttered.

Leswick said, "You might want to take a look through the underbrush. There's a very interesting sight back there out on the path."

Rand turned. He squinted through the tangled bushes in the direction Leswick was pointing. For a moment he saw nothing unusual. Then he did, and he shivered at the sight.

"They aren't pretty, are they?" Leswick asked.

They were hideous. They were four-legged animals the size of wolves, lean and grim. Their heads and rumps were held high; their backs curved down in the middle. They were padding along silently, one after another in a long row.

There must have been hundreds of the vicious-looking beasts in the parade. Each one grasped in his mouth the tail of the one just in front, to keep the pack close together.

Their lips were drawn back in a terrifying grin. Teeth like daggers were on display. Each beast had four long fangs with needle-sharp points. At the side of their mouths jutted yellow-green tusks, broad and flattened like shovels, but sharp as razors along the edges.

The animals were dirty white in color, with bulging blue-rimmed eyes. Their heavy fur was filthy, matted, stinking. Even at this distance, Rand could sense their overpowering rotten odor.

They were killers—a pack of hunters, parading through the jungle. Rand shuddered at the thought of what might have happened to him and Leswick and Dombey, if they had been out there and on the path when the parade came by.

"What if they pick up our scent?" Rand whispered.

"No worry," Dombey said. "They stick to the

path. We're okay in here, I bet. They been passing for a couple minutes now, and nobody's even looked at us."

Dombey spoke calmly. He didn't seem to have any doubts that he was right. He didn't look very impressed with himself, either, for having guessed that deadly beasts were nearby. But how had he known it would be dangerous to stay on the path?

Another wild hunch that wasn't so wild?

Could be, Rand thought. Whatever the reason, Dombey's hunches had saved them twice today from death in the jungle. The other time his hunch hadn't been right. But it hadn't been wrong by much, for the wolf-beasts had showed up right after lunch.

Dombey said, "I think you better let me walk first, boss. I think you better let me be the one to say when we stop, when we go on."

"What you're saying is, you want to take charge."

"That's right, boss."

It hurt Rand's pride to be pushed aside like this. He had been calling the shots up till now, ever since they first boarded the lifeship. And he thought he had done a pretty good job.

But now they were in the jungle. And Dombey seemed to *understand* the jungle, in some weird way. Maybe he didn't have much of an education, but book-learning didn't count for much here.

76

Dombey knew the jungle the way Rand knew machinery and electronic gear.

Maybe Dombey deserves to be running the expedition, from here on in, Rand thought.

It was a little like putting a child in charge. An overgrown child. A child who might just be the best leader in this jungle, though.

Rand knew he didn't have much choice, anyway. Dombey had the muscle to take over, whether Rand liked it or not. He had just shown that, back by the path. The smart thing to do was to give in gracefully.

"All right, Dombey. You're the top man, now," Rand said. "You lead the way. Get us to the beacon."

"Okay, boss."

"You better not call me boss any more. You're the boss now."

"Whatever you say, boss."

Dombey turned and looked through the thick underbrush. Without glancing back, he signaled to Rand and Leswick with his hand.

"Come on," he called. "Animals are gone. Back to the path, now. You can leave all that fruit here," he said to Leswick. "We'll find plenty more."

He led them in cautious single file through the thicket to the main path. Rand brought up the rear, taking the position that Dombey had had.

They walked a little way. Then Rand began to feel funny. He broke out in a strange sweat and his stomach started to complain.

The heat's getting me, he told himself.

But the heat didn't seem to bother Leswick or Dombey. Rand was uneasy about that. Maybe it's because of the fight, he thought. But I shouldn't get sick to my stomach from a fight.

He walked on another hundred feet. Suddenly he was shivering. His legs felt wobbly.

He stopped and called to the others. "Wait a minute. I'm feeling kind of—"

Rand doubled up with cramps. His head was spinning and his skin felt as if it had caught fire. He dropped to his knees and realized he was going to be very sick.

His lunch left him in a hurry.

When he was finished throwing up, he didn't feel quite so bad. He got up slowly, shaking a little. Dombey handed him a canteen and he took a deep pull of water.

"Better now, boss?"

"Better," Rand said hoarsely.

"I guess you should have left them berries alone, back there. I had a hunch that place wasn't no good."

"Is that what your hunch was? That the berries were bad to eat?"

"Sort of," Dombey admitted.

Angrily Rand said, "Then why didn't you speak up? You saw me eat them! You could have said something!"

"Gosh, boss, you were sore at me for telling you not to stop there! I figured I better stop buttin' in!"

"Okay," Rand said sourly. "Okay. I guess I had that coming to me. But from now on, when you see trouble coming, don't keep the news to yourself."

"I won't, any more," Dombey said.

Rand didn't feel very proud of himself. Dombey had really fixed him! Letting him eat those berries when his hunch told him they were bad! Well, I can't blame him, Rand told himself. I laughed at his hunches. So he let me find out about that clearing my own way.

The sickness had gone. It was a lucky thing he had only eaten a handful of berries. More than that might have really made him sick. Or poisoned him, maybe.

Rand kept quiet, now, as they marched along. He admired the graceful way Dombey moved through the dense forest. Dombey's size didn't cause any troubles for him. He always seemed to find the right opening in the curtain of hanging vines that blocked the way.

That nickname of "Tarzan" was the right one, Rand saw. Dombey was really at home here in the jungle. It seemed as natural to him as water was for a fish.

Rand found out why, toward nightfall. Dombey picked a place to stop for the night, and they pitched camp. Using gestures more than words, Dombey showed them the safest places to put their sleeping bags.

Leswick said, "Where did you pick up all this jungle lore, Dombey? You didn't learn it on a space-ship."

"Learned it before I went to space," he said. "Grew up on Hothouse. That planet, it's got some pretty good jungles too."

"Why did you leave?" Rand asked.

Dombey grinned. "Got tired of jungle," he said. "Signed up as a spacehand."

"You should have told me you were an expert on jungle life," Rand said.

"You didn't ask," Dombey told him.

They had a good dinner that night. Dombey climbed a tree and caught half a dozen little squir-rel-like animals. Then he discovered a plant with fat, fleshy roots that turned out to make tasty eat-ing. After they ate, they crawled into their sleeping bags beside the fire. Rand took a reading on the detector before sacking out.

The jungle noises were as loud that night as they had been the night before. Somehow Rand didn't mind them as much, though. He was too tired to worry about anything. He closed his eyes and drifted off into deep sleep.

Not without some bad dreams, though. Dreams of long green arms rising from a brook. Dreams of ugly, snorting animals with long teeth parading through the jungle. Dreams of monsters far more nightmarish than those.

He woke up a couple of times, imagining that they were being attacked. He lay awake for a while, listening to the grunts and growls and hisses and screeches coming from every direction. Then he fell asleep once more.

11

A DAY and a night went by, and all was well. During the day they walked until they were exhausted. At night they camped, built a fire and rested. Rand let Dombey run the whole show. He was still unhappy over the way Dombey had pushed him aside. But he had to admit that the big jetmonkey was doing a good job so far.

They were making better time now. One reason was that Dombey had decided to dump much of the gear Rand had insisted on carrying. They just didn't need all those pots and pans. They didn't even need the water purifier. Rand hadn't used it at all. There were plenty of streams here, and nobody had gotten sick from drinking from them.

It was a lot easier to march, now that they were down to nothing but essentials.

Dombey was staying on course. They were still heading east, and they were still going toward the beacon. A couple of times that day, Rand checked the detector he had rigged, to make sure of that.

Then things started getting a little messy.

When Rand woke up the next morning he heard a funny sound coming from nearby. It sounded like something scratching around in his knapsack.

He opened his eyes, rolled over, had a look.

Something *was* scratching in his knapsack.

It was a long, skinny animal, not much bigger than a cat. Rand saw its furry back half sticking out of the knapsack. The animal had thick greenish fur that looked a bit moldy, and a long pink tail without any fur on it at all.

"Hey," Rand said quietly. "Get out of there!"

The animal didn't pay any attention. It was deep in the knapsack, munching on something.

Rand tugged on the long pink tail. The animal went on munching. He tugged harder. Nothing happened. He tugged even harder than that.

This time, the animal must have felt annoyed. Slowly, tail first, it wriggled its way out, turned around, and gave Rand a cold, fishy stare.

Its head was long and narrow, with a lean snout sticking forward in front for about six inches. Its ears were huge and stood straight up. It had four eyes, arranged in two rows of two just back of the snout. Each of the eyes moved by itself. Each of the eyes looked at Rand from a slightly different angle.

Electronic gear was dangling out of the creature's mouth. Resistors, capacitors, leads, plugs. It had been making a nice meal out of—

"The detector!" Rand shouted, waking up Leswick and Dombey. "Hey, you thing, you've been eating the detector!"

In sudden anger he grabbed for the animal. Nothing doing: the creature slithered back, threw Rand one more sad look, and vanished into the jungle. Rand saw the bare rat-like tail give a final wriggle as it disappeared.

He yanked the detector out of the knapsack. The instrument was in ruins. The animal had pushed it open, somehow—maybe with that long snout—and had chewed up half the components inside. Rand stared at the torn-up circuits in horror.

"Something wrong?" Leswick asked.

"Nothing much. We've lost our detector, that's all."

"What happened?"

Rand explained. He also explained that they didn't have any equipment to replace what had been chewed up. "From here on in," he said, "we've got to travel by guesswork. We don't have any way of finding out where the rescue beacon is exactly. We just know it's somewhere east of here."

"We'll find it," Dombey said.

"Sure," Rand said. "Maybe it'll take us three hundred years, but we'll find it. If we have to march back and forth over this planet forever, we'll find it. Great!"

84

"Was the detector really that important?" Leswick asked.

Rand shrugged. "Without it, I think we'll still come within twenty miles or so of the beacon. After that, I don't know. We'll have to search every square foot of the jungle and trust to our luck."

"We been having pretty good luck so far," Dombey said. "We'll make out okay."

"I wish I felt as sure about that as you do," said Rand.

But there was no way to fix the detector, and nothing to do except hit the road and trust to their luck. They had breakfast and got moving.

Dombey turned in a good job again that day.

He proved once more that he was a genius at finding food. He discovered fruits, nuts, roots, and shoots for them to eat. Sometimes he picked something that turned out not to taste so good, but not often. He caught small animals for their dinners. It was amazing to see how quick he was with his hands.

He led them around some nasty dangers, too. Dombey seemed to have some magic knack of knowing how to stay out of trouble in the jungle. Rand tried to look carefully, but he never saw half the things Dombey noticed.

Such as the almost invisible spiderwebs stretching across the path—put there by giant spiders as

85

big as rabbits, lurking in wait. Such as armies of hungry little animals no bigger than ants, able to devour creatures of any size. Such as dangling vines that weren't vines at all, but snakes.

Dombey spotted these perils and others, before anything serious could happen. And so Rand didn't begrudge him the leadership. Rand kept quiet and did whatever Dombey told him to do.

But on the third day they ran into a situation that was too tricky for Dombey to handle.

On the third day they met the natives of the planet called Tuesday.

Dombey had been leading them all morning through a part of the jungle where the path was narrow and overgrown with vines. It was an unusually hot and sticky day. The frequent light showers of rain didn't do anything to cool the three men off.

They came to a place where the path widened into a broad grassy clearing. Dombey took a couple of steps into the clearing. Then he stopped short.

"What is it?" Rand called after him. "What do you see?"

Dombey turned and walked back toward Rand and Leswick. He looked puzzled. He didn't say a word. But he seemed to be telling Rand silently, "This is something for you to handle."

Rand came forward so he could see what lay ahead. A group of strange beings stood in the clearing. They were alien beings, very different from Earthmen in every way.

They looked like walking barrels. Their bodies, a shiny light brown in color, were short and wide. They were flat on top and bottom, without separate heads or necks. Near the upper end of each barrel were three round, staring eyes. Below the eyes was a slit for breathing, and under that was a wide mouth whose corners turned downward in a permanent frown.

The aliens had short arms covered with thick hair, and six long fingers on each hand. Their legs were big and powerful, like the hind legs of kangaroos. Each of the aliens was holding a broad-bladed sword whose edges were jagged with many sharp barbs.

The strangest thing about these beings, Rand thought, was that they were all alike. It wasn't just a very close resemblance. They were absolutely identical to one another. They could all have been stamped out from the same mold.

He looked around the circle. There were thirty or forty of the aliens, each one the twin of the one next to it. Rand couldn't see how they could tell each other apart.

They seemed excited about the arrival of the three Earthmen. They were talking to each other in a great hubbub, waving their arms about. Their voices were dull and droning, like buzzsaws that needed to be oiled.

Quickly Rand turned and unstrapped some of the gear from Dombey's pack. He burrowed through the knapsack-load of pots and pans. Finally he found what he was looking for: the Thorson thought-converter.

The Thorson converter was tremendously valuable to space explorers. It held the key to all unknown languages. The converter was a translating machine that could solve almost any riddle of speech, no matter how alien.

It looked like a long, slim radio receiver. But within it was a highly intelligent electronic brain. The brain studied the sounds of a language and guessed at meanings for certain words that were repeated often. Then it guessed at other words that were less commonly spoken. It was able to put its guesses together so the wrong guesses could be corrected.

A human being might have been able to figure out an alien language that way if he studied it for fifty or eighty years. The Thorson converter needed only a couple of minutes. And it would do a better job in those few minutes than the human being could do in a whole lifetime of years.

Rand switched the converter on and pointed it toward the aliens. "Say a few words, friends," he told them. "Give us some talk-talk, so we can analyze what you're telling us."

The aliens didn't understand what he was saying,

of course. The converter hadn't learned their language yet. But they replied to Rand's words with a series of loud buzzes and clicks and booms.

"That's it," Rand said. "Keep chattering, fellows!"

He made rapid adjustments on the dial of the Thorson converter as they spoke. He slid the guide panel up and down the indicator until he hit the right range. The converter's speaker was giving forth the alien language without a translation. But the converter was starting to figure out some meanings now.

In mid-buzz, the alien language came clear. The converter said:

"Buzzbuz mumbleclick danger hostile-animal stranger-type buzzbuz clickmumble surround with many swords buzzbuz if hostile KILL."

Rand chewed uneasily at his lip. Into the mouthpiece of the converter he said, "We are not hostile. We are friends."

The converter translated that for the alien. "Buzzclick mumblemumble mumblemumble."

The aliens looked puzzled. They didn't sound any more peaceful. They kept on saying, "Surround with swords. Do they threaten us? Strange creatures. We kill?"

Rand searched his mind for some way to prove to the drum-shaped creatures that he and Dombey and Leswick meant no harm. He said, pointing to the sky, "We are from up there. We have fallen from above."

"Strange ones. Dangerous."

"We have no weapons. See, we are without swords!"

"Buzzbuzzbuz. Clickclickclick."

The converter couldn't translate that one. But it sounded unfriendly.

Rand said, "We were riding a great shining bird. The bird died. We fell from the sky. We want to go back to our homes."

"Buzzclick! Clickbuzz!"

"We mean no harm to you," Rand went on.

"Buzz! Click! Boom! BOOM!"

Rand twisted the converter's dial. He tuned it in a little better.

He said, "We come in peace! We are your friends from Earth!"

"Hostile. Threat. Danger. KILL. KILL. KILL."

12

THE ALIENS hadn't budged from their places. They still stood in a half circle, facing the Earthmen. But they were starting to look restless. Some of them were swinging their swords back and forth impatiently.

It looked as though they might charge at any moment. And that cry of "KILL. KILL. KILL." coming out of the converter wasn't exactly encouraging.

Rand saw that Dombey looked pretty restless too. The big jetmonkey seemed to be getting ready for a fight. His huge hands were clenching into fists, unclenching, clenching again.

Shutting off the converter for a moment, Rand said, "Relax, Tarzan. Stop looking so fierce."

"We got to defend ourselves."

"They have swords and we don't," Rand said. "And they outnumber us ten or fifteen to one. Muscle won't help us now, Dombey. This is something we have to talk our way out of."

The aliens were starting to move closer.

Rand turned the converter on again. "We are heading east to find our friends," he said desperately. He pointed to the east. "When we find them, we will leave your world and never return. Do you understand? We want nothing from you. We're not hostile. We want to leave as soon as we find our friends. We want to leave. We are not your enemies."

The buzzing noises continued. They grew louder and sounded more menacing.

Rand tuned the converter again. It gave this translation:

"We are not able to decide what to do with you, strangers. We must ask a higher authority who decides for us. Make no more words, but come with us to our village."

"Very well," Rand said. "Take us to your village."

He turned the converter off. The aliens moved in on them, forming a tight, buzzing circle. Dombey looked as if he wanted to push the aliens away from him.

Rand said, "Do everything they tell us to do, Dombey. Don't complain, don't refuse. Above all, don't touch any of them or look like you want to hit them. Otherwise they'll kill us. *KILL*. You understand that, Dombey?"

The jetmonkey nodded slowly. "Yeah. Yeah, boss, I won't start no fight. But I don't like them. They're no good."

"I don't like them much either, but there are too

many of them to fight. They're armed and we aren't. They can kill us, Dombey. Go where they tell you. Do what they want you to do."

"Okay," Dombey said agreeably. "You're the boss, boss."

Rand looked at Leswick. The metaphysician had said nothing at all for the past five minutes. He had hardly moved through the whole conversation with the aliens. Now he was permitting himself to be shoved along, scarcely noticing. His eyes looked dreamy. He seemed lost in his thoughts.

"What's the matter with you, professor?" Rand asked. "You synthesizing some new cultural phenomena?"

Leswick didn't reply.

"Hey, Leswick! I'm talking to you!"

"Will you keep quiet, Rand?" the metaphysician snapped. Rand had never heard him speak so sharply before. "Let me think this out, will you?"

"You're going to save us through Metaphysical Synthesis?" Rand said sarcastically.

Leswick just glared at him.

"I beg your pardon for interrupting your thoughts," Rand said. "Sorry! Terribly sorry!" The tone of his voice left no doubt how sorry he really was.

The aliens marched them onward through the jungle.

As they neared the village, Rand began to do

some heavy thinking himself. There *had* to be some way out of this! There had to be some way he could show these suspicious aliens that the three Earthmen were no threat to them.

Maybe there was some way of drawing pictures for them, he thought. Show them the blowup of the ship, show them the crash landing of the lifeship, show them the location of the rescue beacon. Make it clear that we just want to hike to the beacon and signal for help so we can go home.

Another possibility was not to try to explain anything. Let them put us in their jail. Or what passes for a jail among them. And then, in the middle of the night, break out and slip away.

We ought to be able to do it. They look like simple sorts—they wouldn't guard us too closely. Dombey can lead us in the dark. That would be easier than trying to explain ourselves to them. Even with the converter, we don't seem to be able to get our ideas across. They're alien. They don't think the way we do. They can't even begin to understand us. And we can't figure them out, either.

What if they do guard us closely, though?

Then we'll just have to figure out a logical way of dealing with them, Rand told himself. But nothing logical came into his mind. And now they were at the alien village.

The village was set in a broad clearing. Trees had

been chopped down for a great distance on all sides, and bright sunlight came through the opening in the jungle. A small stream ran along one side of the settlement.

The place was fantastically busy. Hundreds more of the barrel-shaped aliens were bustling around in a tremendous hurry, every one of them hard at work. Here, four of them were pounding grain. There, eight of them were putting up a new hut. Over there, six others were trimming logs.

The village consisted of row on row of wooden huts, each one just like all the rest. Every hut was about six feet high and five feet wide. That was big enough to hold one alien, no more. Didn't they have families, Rand wondered? Furniture? Possessions? How could they live in such tiny cabins?

The huts were laid out in a carefully designed pattern. The rows were neat and straight, each one containing about twenty-five huts except for the rows near the center of the village. Those were shorter, so that a kind of plaza was formed right in the middle of things.

In the center of the plaza stood a single huge hut. It was of the same design as the others, with a flat top and straight sides, but it was about twenty feet high and twenty feet wide. It towered over the smaller buildings like a strange square skyscraper.

That must be where the "higher authority" of

the village lives, Rand thought. It's a temple, or a palace, or maybe a city hall. It's where the local chief will decide what's going to happen to us.

The aliens were saying something to him. Rand held the thought-converter toward them for the translation.

"You will go to the great house," they were telling him. "We will present you to the Mother."

"Who is the Mother?" Rand asked. But he got no answer.

They walked toward the great house.

He noticed a strange thing: there didn't seem to be any children in the village, or even any young adults. All of the aliens seemed to be of the same age and size and height.

There was another surprise as he got closer to the great house. Up till now, every villager he had seen was busy doing something. Now Rand saw a few loafers. These aliens lay sprawled on the ground looking remarkably lazy. Their eyes were closed, their mouths drooped open, their arms were folded across their middles. They weren't dead, but they weren't very lively, either.

These sleepers had slightly deeper brown skins than the others. Their bodies were soft and flabby. Two or three of them opened their eyes to stare at the Earthmen. But they closed them again after a brief look. All the other villagers were such hard workers. Rand wondered why these lucky few got off so lightly.

They came to the great house, now. Three of the aliens went inside. One of his captors turned to Rand and said, "Clickclick click."

"Say that again?" The machine translated Rand's words into clicks.

The alien repeated the noises into the thought-converter. They came out as, "You wait out here."

"Can't we go inside?"

"Negative negative negative. NO! Strange ones must not enter great house of the Mother. Stay here while we tell about you to the Mother."

Rand shrugged. "If you want us to wait, we'll wait, I guess."

Time passed—one minute, three, five. Rand began to fidget. What was going on in there? Who was the Mother, and what was she telling these people?

He looked at the swords of the aliens who guarded them. He didn't like to think about the wicked-looking barbs along the edges of those blades.

He wondered if their luck was going to run out right here.

Luck had allowed the three of them to survive the explosion aboard the spaceship, when everyone else died. Luck had let them get into the lifeship and make a safe escape. Luck had brought them down on Tuesday unharmed, even though he had never piloted a ship before. Luck had carried them safely through the jungle despite all the hidden dangers.

But now their luck had changed. They were prisoners. Their lives were at the mercy of these alien creatures. Unarmed, outnumbered, they had to depend on the whim of the Mother. Would she spare them? He wondered. They seemed awfully unfriendly.

Another five minutes went by. Then the three aliens who had gone into the great house came out. They buzzed something to the ones who guarded the Earthmen. Rand strained to hear it, but the words were too faint for the converter to pick them up.

Then one of the aliens turned to him and said clearly, "The Mother has decided. You are dangerous. You threaten our safety."

"No," Rand protested. "We don't threaten anybody's safety. We'll leave as soon as we reach our— our friend. Our friend in the east!"

"The Mother says you threaten our safety," the alien said again, firmly. "And so you must die!"

Not here, Rand thought. Not now. Not like this. Not in a sticky jungle on an unknown planet for a stupid reason.

The ring of guards lifted their swords. The cruel

barbs glittered in the hot sunlight. Here it comes, he told himself.

He tried to get ready to die. He was going to go down fighting. Maybe he'd take a few of the barrel-shaped creatures with him.

Then Leswick, who had been silent for a long time, came to life.

"Wait!" he shouted into the converter. "Wait! I demand to see the Mother! I claim the right to return to our hive!"

13

RAND WAS baffled. He did a double take, blinking in surprise, then stared at Leswick. The little man seemed mysteriously changed. His weak eyes were bright, his hands were outspread, his fingers were trembling nervously.

"What did you say?" Rand asked.

"Hush," Leswick muttered. To the aliens he said, "Did you hear me? We have become cut off from our hive. We ask you to let us go back to it."

The aliens were strangely silent for a moment. Then they turned to face each other, and they buzzed and hummed in low tones, talking things over. The converter wasn't able to pick up their words.

Rand realized in that moment what the world of Bill Dombey must be like. Just now, Rand was as bewildered as the big jetmonkey usually was. His mind was blank. He couldn't begin to figure out what Leswick was up to.

All he knew was that Leswick and the aliens seemed to understand each other.

The aliens continued to confer. Leswick kept on

watching them tensely. The sound of his breathing was harsh and rasping.

Finally one of the aliens hopped forward. "It is all different now. We did not understand your trouble," the creature said to Leswick. "We will talk to the Mother again. We will see if she will let you speak with her."

The alien went back into the great house. It was in there about five minutes. Then it came out and announced, "You may enter. The Mother will see you."

Rand started forward. But Leswick reached out and caught his arm.

"No—I'll go in alone. You stay out here and keep Dombey company." Leswick took the converter from him.

"But—" Rand let the word trail off. He saw that he was out of his depth, now. Without argument, he let the Metaphysical Synthesist enter the building. The ring of guards closed tightly around Dombey and Rand after Leswick went in.

Again time passed with terrible slowness. It began to rain again, but only for a few minutes. Insects circled Rand's head and he shooed them away. Now and then the aliens exchanged words. But without the converter Rand could understand nothing.

He looked at Dombey. The huge man stood with his arms folded. He didn't seem to be thinking about anything at all. Dombey wasn't bothered by the mystery of what was going on. Dombey didn't even try to figure out such things. Life is simpler that way, Rand thought.

But he couldn't act that way himself—not with his life at stake. He wanted desperately to know what Leswick was trying to do. Why was he pulling that business about returning to their hive? What hive? Where?

From inside the great house, Leswick called, "Rand, will you come in here now? Better bring Dombey, too."

"Coming," Rand called back. He nudged the jetmonkey. "Let's go in, Tarzan. And remember, stand still, don't touch anything, don't make any trouble."

Dombey grinned. "Sure, boss."

They went in.

The great house was as dark as a tomb inside. The only light came from three small openings in the roof. Faint beams of brightness slanted into the building.

The air had a stale, musty smell. Rand stood just within the entrance until his eyes grew used to the dimness. Then he saw Leswick in the middle of the room. Leswick pointed to something against the far wall.

"This is the Mother of this tribe, Rand," he said.

From the rear of the great house came a dull booming sound. The converter translated it:

"Welcome, strange ones."

Rand looked up and back. At first he saw nothing. Then he spied the Mother, high on the wall. She sat on a wide, deep shelf eight or nine feet above the floor, peering down at them.

She was a strange sight. He had never seen anything so weird before.

The Mother was at least twice the size of the ordinary aliens. Her body was a pale greenish-white color, and it was tremendously swollen. She might have been barrel-shaped like the others, once. But now she hardly had any shape at all. She was just a great mass of wrinkled and bloated flesh.

Her legs were tiny, flimsy things. They could never hold up her immense weight, Rand knew. Her eyes, round and bulging, were the size of dishes. Her mouth was an enormous slit in her huge body. She seemed to be terribly old . . . hundreds, thousands, millions of years old.

The aliens who were guarding the three Earthmen bowed before her. Leswick signaled, and Rand bowed too. Even Dombey got the idea and touched one knee to the floor.

The Mother said, "I am the Mother. You are welcome here, you strangers from another hive. How different you are!"

103

Rand was tongue-tied with awe. He tried to say something, but no words would come. What could you say to a creature like this? She was like something out of a dream.

"Tell the Mother about *our* Mother," Leswick urged him in a dry, insistent voice.

"Our—Mother?" Rand repeated.

"Go ahead, Rand. Tell—her—about—our—Mother. Describe our Mother's wonderful metal body. Speak of our Mother's marvelous thirty-mega-cycle carrier beam."

Rand felt like he was sinking in a quicksand swamp of bewilderment. But only for a moment. Then he caught on and took the hint.

"Yes," he said. "Our Mother is located to the east, many days' journey from here. She is taller than we are, and does not move from the place where she stands. Set in her forehead is an eye of great beauty."

He went on to describe the signal beacon with the most complete details he could supply. As he spoke, his mind protested against the sheer madness of what was taking place. What was the point of making believe that the beacon was their "Mother"? How—

He kept talking until he had run out of things to say.

Then the huge alien being said, "Yes. We know the place and we have seen your Mother. We know her and we have wondered for a long time where her children might be."

"We wish to return to her," Leswick said anxiously. "We did not mean to enter your hive, but we became lost in the jungle. We want nothing more than to finish our journey toward our Mother."

"We understand," came the solemn reply.

"Then you will help us?"

"Yes," the Mother said. "Yes, we will cause our people to guide you to your Mother. We know your sorrow and we take pity upon you, strange ones from another hive."

Leswick dropped to his knees. Rand did the same. Only Dombey remained standing. And then even he, overcome by superstitious awe, lowered himself heavily to the floor.

"We thank you for this kindness, Mother of this hive," said Leswick with great solemnity.

"Yes, we thank you," Rand added.

And Dombey chimed in, loud and clear and deep. "Yeah, thanks, Mother. Thanks."

14

MUCH LATER, Rand began to understand.

These beings were organized much like ants or bees. Although they weren't insects, they had an insect-like type of society. Leswick had guessed it first, and he had been right.

Most of the villagers were workers or soldiers. They were all of the same sex—or rather, they didn't have any sex at all. They never produced young ones. That was why they lived in small huts, one by one.

The Mother was the only member of the tribe who ever had children. She was really and truly the tribe's mother. Just as a queen bee lays all the eggs in the hive, the Mother here gave birth to all the villagers and ruled the tribe.

The fat, sleepy loafers outside the great house were her husbands. They were like the drones or males of a beehive. Their only job was to keep the population of the tribe growing.

No children were in sight in the village because each year's brood was probably hatched at the same time. Very likely the last brood was already full-grown, and the new young ones weren't due yet. All the workers looked the same since they were all produced by the Mother.

It made sense, now that Rand had had some time to think it over. But he wondered how Leswick had figured it out so quickly. And how had the little philosopher known that that stuff about their own "hive" and "Mother" would work?

Certainly the aliens were friendly now. That night they threw a feast for the three Earthmen in the plaza outside the great house of the Mother. The main course was a kind of thick blue-green jelly with a delicious spicy taste.

Afterwards the aliens gave a concert. At least, Rand *thought* it was a concert. A dozen of the barrel-shaped beings lined up in a row and made humming-booming noises for about half an hour. Rand was afraid it would be embarrassing if he asked what they were doing. So when it was over he made a little speech of thanks for the music, and hoped he was right.

The Earthmen slept that night in village huts, one man to a hut. Rand didn't find it pleasant to lie down on the bare dirt floor of the hut. Stray insects kept wandering across it and him. The hut had no windows, and the air was hot and stuffy inside. But he knew he had to be polite. He and Dombey and Leswick were guests here. They had to accept the hospitality of the aliens.

In the morning, ten of the villagers escorted them into the jungle. Five marched in front of them, five in back. They carried their swords in their hands, ready for trouble.

At a steady pace they led the three wanderers farther toward the east. Toward the rescue signal beacon. Toward their Mother.

Rand was depressed and upset despite himself. At first he couldn't understand what was bothering him. They hadn't been harmed by the aliens, had they? They had come through the dangers in good shape. They even had gained a team of guides to take them to the beacon.

So why did he feel so miserable?

He realized why, after a while. It was because Leswick, not Tom Rand, had got them safely through the village. Leswick, for whom he felt only scorn and contempt. Leswick, the phony philosopher. Leswick had handled the situation beautifully. Rand hadn't been able to do a thing.

I was so proud of myself, Rand thought. I got us off the *Clyde F. Bohmer* okay. I got us down here to Tuesday okay. I built a detector and a water purifier. I was the clever boy, I was the one the others couldn't survive without.

But it took Dombey to get us through the jungle.

And it took Leswick to deal with the aliens.

In mid-morning, when they were far from the village, Rand said to Leswick, "Tell me something."

"Such as?"

"How did you know the aliens were what they were? And how did you know what would make them let us go?"

The Metaphysical Synthesist smiled mildly. "How did I *know?* That's a tricky word, Rand. It means different things to you and me. To you, it's impossible to *know* anything unless you can feel it and measure it and calculate from it."

"And you?"

Leswick shrugged. "I work from intuition. Hunches. I don't need every last scrap of evidence there is, before I make up my mind. I jump to conclusions. For you, one and one always make two. For me, one and one can make three, five, seventeen—it all depends on the situation."

"Wonderful. But what's the good of that? One and one *don't* make seventeen!"

"Not in any logical way, no," said Leswick. "Logic isn't the only way to think, though. When we were in the village I was collecting facts about those people. Adding up things about their way of life. And suddenly—in a flash of intuition—I saw the answer. I *knew* the answer."

"And Dombey *knew* there would be those wolf-things parading down the path, I suppose," Rand said sourly. "Which is why he beat the blazes out of me while you stood by grinning."

"It was the only way to get you to accept the evidence," Leswick said. "There wasn't time for further discussion. So Dombey had to use his fists, or the wolves would have caught up with us. And in the village, I spoke up when I saw the answer. I couldn't wait to talk it over with you—not with those swords already coming close."

"I still can't see any of this, Leswick. This guess-work."

"I know you can't. You still prefer logic. Well, your nice neat logic would have turned you into wolf-meat back there. Logic wouldn't have helped you against those barbed swords, either. And logic wouldn't have been much good in *this* situation, either."

Leswick pointed ahead. The jungle path was splitting. One fork went off to the left, the other to the right.

Which fork led to the beacon?

The aliens knew. They turned off to the left, and the Earthmen followed.

Rand's cheeks grew hot and red. Score another point for Leswick, he thought. Without the alien guides, they would have become lost here, now that the detector was no good. He wouldn't have known which fork to take. And it was Leswick who had gained the guides for them.

"I just don't get it," Rand went on. "You guessed that the aliens had a society like that of bees. Okay. And it was clever of you to figure out that the Mother was like a queen bee. And to get her sympathy by claiming that the beacon was our Mother, that we were returning to the hive. But how could you *tell?* How did you know what angles to try?"

"You haven't studied Metaphysical Synthesis, have you?" Leswick asked suddenly.

"I know a little about it. But—"

"You know enough about it not to like it. But not enough to understand it, obviously—or you'd know how I got my answers."

"You got them through intuition," Rand said. "That's all Metaphysical Synthesis is. Hunches. Guesswork."

"That's part of it," Leswick admitted. "The base." He grinned. "But Dombey's something of a Metaphysical Synthesist too, even if he can't pronounce the words. Ask him what *his* methods of figuring things out are, some time. Ask him what kind of logic he uses."

Suddenly Rand got tired of the discussion. He didn't like where it was heading.

"Skip it," he said. "You made your point."

15

LATE THE next day the aliens in front of them stopped short in the path. They began to point and cry out in loud thumping sounds.

"It's the rescue beacon!" Rand said. "We've reached the beacon!"

"Give me the converter," Leswick told him.

Rand switched the instrument on and handed it to the philosopher. Leswick walked forward. The beacon was a tall metal cone standing in a little opening in the forest.

"There is our Mother," Leswick announced loudly. "We thank you for your help. You must go back now. You may not approach our Mother more closely."

For good measure he made the announcement twice more. The aliens bent low to pay respects to the Mother of the Earthmen.

"We wish you well, strange ones," one of them said. "We hope you return soon to your hive. Farewell."

"Farewell, and thanks," Leswick said.

The aliens backed away into the jungle and began to move down the path toward their village. In a few minutes there was no sign of them. The three Earthmen stood together in front of the beacon.

The beacon was an impressive gadget. Rand could see why the aliens might think it was alive. Its bright red pilot light looked like a giant eye. Mounted around its middle were infrared heat-rays to keep the jungle growth from getting too close. Every few weeks the heat-rays turned themselves on, cooking any plant life that was starting to sprout. The beacon was huge, gleaming, awesome.

"So we made it," Leswick said. "There was a time when I was sure we'd never get here."

"When was that?" asked Rand.

"When you were leading us in the jungle. I wondered if Dombey and I were going to get control over you in time. Before you fouled us all up, that is. You stopped being of much use about the time we landed on this planet, Rand. You were nothing but a drag—nothing but dead weight."

"That's kind of you to tell me."

"It's true, though. I mean that logic and technical knowhow can get people only so far."

Rand scowled. He had tried to run everything as logically and intelligently as he could. But somehow he had come out of the journey looking to Leswick and Dombey like a total idiot. He knew that he wouldn't have made it here alive without both of them.

"Are you saying that logical thinking is worthless?" he asked.

Leswick shook his head. "Logical thinking is necessary and valuable, Rand. But it doesn't take you the whole journey. In the jungle, we needed sheer animal instinct. Dombey had it. You didn't. Dombey can't do solid geometry, but he's got survival ability."

"I suppose so."

"And in dealing with an alien race, logic doesn't always work too well either. Not if *they* don't think logically too. We needed a kind of logic-plus-intuition. Guesswork, if you like the word. And that's what Metaphysical Synthesis trains people to use."

Rand was silent. He kicked the ground in annoyance.

For the first time in his life, he felt his faith in his own ability waver. He had always been so confident that he could take care of himself, no matter what.

Not here, though.

How smug I was! I thought I was the all-important man! I thought Dombey was a dope and Leswick was a fraud. And I'd be dead without both of them now.

It hurt to think about it. Especially when he remembered how he had been putting the other two down, at the beginning. How he had congratulated himself again and again for his brains and his cleverness.

"Well?" Leswick asked.

"Well what?"

"How long are you going to stand there daydreaming?" the little man asked impatiently. "There's the rescue beacon, you know."

Rand still paused, tied up in his thoughts.

"We're waiting for you," Leswick said. "You don't think *I* know how to operate a *machine*, do you?"

It sounded sarcastic. Maybe it was. Rand smiled faintly and stepped forward to the signal beacon.

The beacon showed signs of half a century's exposure to the weather. But generally it was in fine shape. Its metal skin was clear and shiny except for a few stains and scratches. The pilot light was on, proving that the beacon was in working order.

Operating the beacon wasn't really very hard. Even Leswick could have done it. There was a big button in the middle of the beacon's side. Under it was a long label that declared in many languages:

PRESS TO TALK

Rand pressed the button.

That switched on a special-space transmitter. The transmitter sent an alarm signal to the nearest rescue station.

Almost instantly a deep voice said, "Rescue service speaking. State your name and location."

"This is Space Engineer Tom Rand, of Earth. I'm on a planet called Tuesday in the system of star number GGC 8788845."

"Okay," said the Rescue Service man. "I've got you plotted on my chart already. How'd you get there?"

"I was on the *Clyde F. Bohmer*. The overdrive blew up and destroyed the ship."

"Yeah, I know. It's down on the rescue list."

"I escaped in a lifeship and landed here," Rand said.

"You're the first *Bohmer* survivor to call in. We'll have a rescue ship your way in a day or two. You all alone?"

"No," Rand said. "I'm with Anthony Leswick and William Dombey. As far as I know, the three of us are the only survivors."

The voice at the other end was silent for a moment. "Leswick . . . Dombey. . . . I've got the *Bohmer*'s passenger list right here. Yeah, here they are. Dombey's a crewman, huh? Leswick . . . Dombey. . . . A metaphysical whatsit and a jet-monkey. You must have had a heck of a rough time with those two, huh?"

"It wasn't bad," Rand said.

"I mean, running a lifeship with all that dead weight aboard. And afterwards. Couple of guys like that, they must have been pretty useless when things got tight. A lot of good those two must have been! Dead weight!"

Rand frowned. He looked around at Dombey and Leswick, who weren't close enough to hear what was being said. He thought of trying to explain things to the Rescue Service man. Trying to tell him how it *really* had been.

What was the use? The other man would never understand.

"Yeah," Rand said quietly. "All that dead weight!"

ROBERT SILVERBERG is a free-lance writer familiar to most science-fiction enthusiasts for *Planet of Death, Time of the Great Freeze, Conquerors From the Darkness,* and *The Gate of Worlds.* A graduate of Columbia University, Mr. Silverberg has written science-fiction for both adults and young people, and served as President of the Science Fiction Writers of America for the 1967–68 term. He is also the author of many books dealing with archaeology and history, including *The Man Who Found Nineveh* and *To the Rock of Darius.* Mr. Silverberg and his wife and several pet cats live in New York in an old Riverside house that was once the home of Mayor Fiorello LaGuardia.

J
SIL

Silverberg, Robert

Three survived

© THE BAKER & TAYLOR CO.